THE MANY ADVENTURES OF MEILIN

THE MONKEY KING'S
DAUGHTER

BOOK #2

T. A. DEBONIS

PUBLISHED BY:
Todd A. DeBonis • DVTVFilm
The Monkey King's Daughter®, is a registered trademark of Todd A. DeBonis

ISBN: 978-0-9678094-2-7 (0-9678094-2-8)

REGISTERED: US Library of Congress, WGA, USPTO

COVER ILLUSTRATION: John Forcucci, ©2009

WEBSITE: TheMonkeyKingsDaughter.com

ACKNOWLEDGMENTS: Once again, I'm extremely grateful to John Forcucci for his brilliant cover art, Monty Haas and Laurie Joy Haas for their diligent proofing, and all three for their overwhelming encouragement, support and longtime friendship. I also want to thank my neighbor, Gang Liu, for his careful translation of the Mandarin lullaby contained in this story. Most importantly, I want to thank my wife, Lien, for giving me the time to make all this happen—anh yêu em mãi mãi.

PRINTED IN THE USA

For my two girls,
My-Linh and Anna

Chapter 1

Meilin Cheng did her best to parry the lightning fast attacks Master Zhang dealt. His thin yew switch struck her repeatedly on her legs, her arms, and her ribcage—all in rapid succession without contest. The blows stung, as Master Zhang intended, but did no real damage. With disgust, the two-thousand-year-old Taoist Master stopped and glared at her.

"What *are* you thinking about!" he demanded.

"I don't know," Meilin answered sheepishly. The slight 14-year-old Asian American averted her eyes and stared at the matted grassy ground of the small mountainside field they were standing in. Indeed, what *was* she thinking about? Moreover, *why* was she there? She was there to train—at least that was the plan. Just because she fought well alongside her father, Sun

Wukong, the Monkey King, when she and her Uncle Zhu Bajie entered the Gate that transported them back in time to mythical China a few months ago to save her mother from the evil Demon Bull King, that did not make her a warrior. It made her lucky. Sure she inherited most, if not all, of her father's ability and power, but without purpose—or focus, her innate ability was useless to her. Only when she went *full monkey*, as she called it when she transformed into her demon monkey state, did her abilities take over.

But that wasn't what this was about. She needed to be able to call upon her skills without transforming out of her human state. And that would take training—lots of training.

"I guess I'm just not into it today," Meilin offered.

"*Into it!*" Master Zhang snorted. "This isn't something you're *into* on a whim! If this was a sword," he said, referring to the switch in his hand, "you'd be dead! Then what? You're not immortal, Princess!"

"Yes, Sifu," Meilin replied, bowing to her teacher. She cringed at the title *Princess*. It was not a title she wanted or enjoyed, even if it was true—she *was* Princess of the Monkey Kingdom, like it or not. "I'm sorry. It's just that I've got midterms coming up and..."

"Silence!" Master Zhang barked. "No excuses. The lesson's over!"

"Sifu, please..."

But Master Zhang was already done with her. "I promised your father I'd train you. For me to do that, you must *want* to be trained. When your mind is clear of these things you call *midterms* or whatever other excuses you have—return. Until then..." Master Zhang raised his hand, directing Meilin to part his presence.

Meilin's heart sank, but there was nothing she could do or say that would change her teacher's mind.

Meilin bowed with both her hands clasped, but the white-haired old Taoist had already turned away, heading for the tranquility of his tiny mountainside cottage.

Meilin exhaled with heavy disappointment, not with Master Zhang—but with herself. The old man was right—she *was* distracted. Was it really about her upcoming midterm exams, or was something else on her mind?

Meilin willed her magical jade bo staff to shrink back to its usual chopstick-size and poked it into her ponytail knot next to the two shorter hair sticks already there. Her three jade hair sticks were a gift from her grandmother, Guanyin, Goddess of Mercy. They were also the keys to the Gate that transported Meilin from her uncle Zhu Bajie's modest *Heavenly River Imports* antique shop in downtown Midland Hills, California, over three thousand years back in time to the magical era of Sun Wukong, the Jade Emperor, and the rest of the Chinese pantheon.

The staccato sound of a pair of clapping hands interrupted Meilin's train of thought.

Meilin whirled in place. From the edge of the bamboo forest that surrounded the clearing, a Huli-jing emerged. Meilin recognized the strikingly beautiful demon fox instantly. She was the Huli-jing scout she met at her Uncle Sha Wujing's camp during her first sojourn to the past.

Meilin was immediately cautious. Huli-jings were not to be trusted, though this one seemed to be loyal to her Uncle Sha. Still, one could never be certain.

The Huli-jing approached Meilin. She appeared to be unarmed, though with a Huli-jing you could never be certain about that either. They were masters of the shadow arts and exceedingly cunning—like a fox, from which the expression could well have originated.

Meilin could feel her body tingle, a precursor to morphing into her demon monkey state. She did her best to suppress the sensation.

"Well done, Princess," the Huli-jing continued, clapping twice more for effect. "It takes quite a bit of work to tick-off Master Zhang. You've done it in a matter of minutes."

"Let me guess—Uncle Sha sent you to keep an eye on me," Meilin stated with some annoyance, referring to the demon sand monk who was one of her father's closest companions.

"Hardly," the demon fox said. "Now that Bull King's been routed from the land and Balance restored, Sha Wujing has little need of my services."

"Then why are you here?" Meilin asked.

"Perhaps I was just passing through," the Huli-jing said casually, now standing mere inches from Meilin.

The demon fox was at least a foot taller than Meilin, forcing her to look upward into the Huli-jing's piercing black eyes. For all her beauty, Meilin could detect an unsettling coldness in the vixen's gaze.

"Or perhaps I came to collect the reward that's still on your head," the demon fox continued, as she moved to Meilin's right and began to circle the teen. "It's up to 100 thousand pieces of gold now."

"Is that all?" Meilin said, forcing an air of nonchalance into her voice.

"I like your hair," the Huli-jing remarked, suddenly reaching up to touch Meilin's ponytail knot—and her jade hair sticks.

Meilin half-turned in place, her own hand moving faster, intercepting the Huli-jing's wrist before she could touch her.

"I like yours, too," Meilin returned, measuring the sinewy strength of the Huli-jing's forearm. Meilin could feel that the demon fox was powerful, yet there was no hint of menacing energy welling in the demon fox's limb.

"You really must tell me the name of the conditioner you use," Meilin continued.

The demon fox eyed Meilin for a long moment. Her face then broke into a smile. "I like you," she said, retracting her hand and stepping back. "I can tell we're going to be friends."

"Cool," Meilin replied. "Can't have enough friends. Unfortunately, I gotta go..." Meilin took a step toward her worn school backpack that lay on the ground near the Huli-jing's feet. Before Meilin could grab it, the demon fox picked it up. The zipper was open and she peered inside.

"Are you a scholar?" the Huli-jing asked, casually flipping through the numerous books.

"Hardly. Those are my school books," Meilin replied, holding her arm out for her backpack. "Even though my mom lets me come here for the weekends, she still expects me to study."

"Why?" the demon fox asked.

"I ask myself that same question—usually right before a big test," Meilin smiled, still waiting for the demon fox to hand over her backpack.

"Eng...lish. Che...Che..." the curious Huli-jing attempted.

"Chemistry," Meilin interjected, pronouncing the subject for her.

"Hmph!" the Huli-jing shrugged as she finally handed the backpack over. "Your world must be very different from this one."

"That's for sure!" Meilin chuckled. Meilin slung the backpack over her shoulder. She then conjured a small cloud at her feet. It lifted her up off the grass, putting her at eye level with the demon fox.

"Well, gotta fly if I'm gonna make it home in time for dinner. Nice to see you again," Meilin said.

The Huli-jing nodded.

"Oh, I almost forgot—what's your name?" Meilin asked, before leaving.

The Huli-jing seemed slightly surprised at Meilin's question, as if no one had ever asked her for her name before.

"Xiao-Hong," she answered.

"Xiao-Hong," Meilin repeated. "It's pretty. Okay, Xiao-Hong, see you next time..." And with that, Meilin flew up into the sky on her cloud and headed east toward the Huaguo Mountains.

The demon fox watched Meilin disappear from view. When she was gone, the Huli-jing gazed down at the item in her hand that she secretly pilfered from Meilin's backpack—a small magenta *iPod nano*. She gazed at it, not knowing what it was or what it did, but it was shiny and pretty. Xiao-Hong turned the video MP3 player over in her hands. On the back was engraved *Meilin & Jessie, Best Friends Forever.*

The Huli-jing's expression turned cold as her hand closed around the tiny device. She then dropped it into a pocket inside her robe, morphed back into her red-grey fox form, and slipped silently back into the forest.

Chapter 2

Mount Huaguo quickly came into view as Meilin soared across the sky on her traveling cloud. From an altitude of 5000 feet, the mountain range lived up to its name—*The Mountain of Flowers and Fruit.* The steep and rugged slopes were lush and green, decorated with every exotic fruit and colorful flora one could imagine. It was no wonder that this was the home of the Monkey Kingdom. And, cut into the base of the mountain, masked by a breathtaking 1500-foot waterfall, was Shuiliandong—the fabled *Water-Curtain Cave* her father boldly entered over 800 years ago to prove himself worthy to rule all monkey-kind.

Meilin could feel a now familiar tension rise within as she began her descent. Far below, the rocky banks of the large pool of churning water created by the tumultuous waterfall, was filled with scores of laughing and frolicking monkey-like children of all ages. This was the heart of her father's kingdom. And though these were technically her relatives, she still wasn't used to walking among them. To further complicate her mixed feelings was the fact that everyone there, especially the children, adored her. She was the Monkey King's daughter—Princess Meilin—a title and position she was still struggling to come to grips with.

Perhaps it was the word *monkey* that she couldn't get past. Yet these weren't *monkey-monkeys*—like in a twenty-first century zoo. These were demon monkeys, very much like people. And yet they weren't people. Maybe *that* was the crux of the matter. Meilin still couldn't accept the fact that she was a half-breed. She wasn't half-human either. Her mother was born of the Chinese fairy-folk. So what did that really make her? By modern Midland Hills, California standards, it made her a freak of nature. It was *Identity Crisis 101* and she was failing it miserably.

What was equally odd was the fact that *who* she was—and *what* she was—didn't amount to a hill of beans to her best friend, Jessie. She was the only one who knew Meilin's secret. She was also the only one Meilin could trust not to tell.

In fact, Jessie Macintyre rather enjoyed making the trip through the Gate with Meilin, traveling back in time to the Monkey Kingdom. At least she did now.

Jessie's first trip through the Gate was quite traumatic and she did freak out when she saw Meilin's uncle Zhu Bajie morph into his true form—that of the legendary, Pigsy the Pig. But that was over a month ago when Meilin exposed her to the full truth as she promised. Now, she accepted most everything she saw as normal. Even the flying didn't faze her. And if Jessie could accept things the way they were, why couldn't Meilin?

Was it because Jessie knew she was 100 percent human? That when she returned home to her real world, she fit in? Was that what was really bothering Meilin—the feeling that she didn't belong to either of the two worlds she lived in?

When Meilin landed near the water's edge, she was immediately greeted with the happy cries of *"Meilin! Meilin!"* from the scores of monkey-children that surrounded her. Many of them carried freshly-picked flowers that they tried to press into her hands. Some offered her the large fresh figs that they were already eating. Meilin put on her happy face and returned their smiles. She even forced herself to ruffle the hair of several of the monkey-boys that scampered around her, though in fact, she felt uncomfortable doing so. For some reason she didn't understand, she didn't like touching their fur—which was crazy, she knew. These were her kin. Their fur was no different than hers when she morphed into her demon monkey state. So what was the problem?

When she first "discovered" who and what she was when her powers manifested on her fourteenth birthday, this wasn't an issue. Saving her mother was the issue. But in the weeks that followed after the first adventure that changed her life forever, the anxiety of her dual identity began to creep in.

Meilin even had to back off on her abilities with regard to her high school's JV volleyball team. She could have easily and single-handedly led her team to the state championship. But that would have drawn too much attention to her—the one thing she absolutely couldn't afford. So she had to feign injury and let the other girls take over.

That put her nemesis Tiffany Edwards back in the limelight—and back on Meilin's case. The team came in fourth place in their league. Respectable, but not what they envisioned with Meilin as their star middle hitter. But that was what Meilin needed to happen. She needed the protection of anonymity and if that meant she would have to commit social suicide—so be it. Tiffany was free to resume picking on her, and she did—it was in her nature. But Tiffany was wary now, never really sure anymore how far she could push Meilin—which in this case, was exactly how Meilin needed it to be.

Meilin wanted to discuss her concerns with her mother or her Uncle Z. But her mother was preoccupied with thoughts of her father. And Uncle Z, well... even though he was a lovable and wise demon pig, he was still a guy and this was ultimately a girl thing. So that left her with her best friend—Jessie. And even though Jessie told Meilin countless times to quit trying to psychoanalyze every little thing that came up— she just couldn't. For Jessie, having a friend with incredible powers was cool. She couldn't see the downside. But for Meilin, the one who had to live it, the downside was plain as day.

The swirling water in the pool at her feet suddenly broke as Jessie surfaced for air.

"Hey! You're back early!" Jessie said, hauling herself out of the crystal clear water.

The brown-haired teen snatched up her yellow beach blanket that lay on the broad flat rocks and wrapped it around her shoulders. "Brr," she shivered. "That mountain water is ice cold—but feels great! How about a dip?"

Meilin shook her head, no. "Time to go."

"Aw, really? It's still early," Jessie protested.

"Sorry," Meilin replied, turning to make her way along the rocky banks for the base of the waterfall.

"Didn't go so good, huh?" Jessie said, quickly gathering up her suntan lotion, sunglasses, and her own magenta *iPod nano*.

"Nope," Meilin returned gruffly.

The two girls hopped up the rocks on the left side of the waterfall in order to access the precarious banana leaf-covered bamboo monkey bridge the demon monkeys constructed to allow easy entry to Water Curtain Cave without getting wet.

The demon monkey guards bowed their heads with respect as Meilin walked past their posts. The Huaguo Mountains were home to many demon-folk, not just the Monkeys. Much of its mysteries were still undiscovered. That meant that as powerful as the Monkey nation was, they needed to remain vigilant. Only a fool would have designs on Sun Wukong's kingdom—but as history has often shown, there was never a shortage of fools.

The interior of Water Curtain Cave was as spectacular as the waterfall that concealed it. The main cavern was huge and extended far back into the mountain. Its massive and fabulously-shaped crystalline stalactites hung from the ceiling rock like long glittering icicles. Its equally colorful and fantastic mounds of stalagmites sprouted from the cavern floor everywhere.

Towards the center rear, atop a stone dais, was her father's throne. It was simple in design, made of oak and hickory. Her uncle Zhu Bajie often joked that he'd have it replaced with a *La-Z-Boy Recliner*, but the joke went unappreciated, since no one there knew or cared what a *La-Z-Boy* was.

What *was* new to the cave was the Gate. Sun Wukong had Guanyin's creation removed from the Jade Emperor's Heavenly Palace and transported to Shuilian-dong, for both security and convenience. The Monkey King wanted it available for his wife and daughter's use at all times. He also wanted it guarded at all times, and that meant by warriors of his own kind.

As Meilin and Jessie approached the Gate, courtiers shooed away the train of monkey-children that trailed after them.

Meilin took the three jade hair sticks from her hair and placed them in the lock. The lock instantly opened and the Gate activated, creating the magical vortex that would transport Jessie and herself into the future, back to the very same

Gate she was now entering, located in her Uncle Z's shop.

The scores of demon monkey children shouted *"goodbye"* and *"hurry back"* in their high-pitched monkey-voices and waved vigorously.

Meilin and Jessie turned and waved back to them before stepping into the vortex. This was one of the joys Meilin wanted desperately to fully embrace, but couldn't. The love and affection from children, demon or human, was pure and honest. She only wished that her own heart could reciprocate with the same freedom. In time, she hoped, it would.

- - - - -

Xiao-Hong ran swiftly and silently through the bamboo forest. The onset of dusk didn't affect the Huli-jing's vision as she negotiated the tall stalks that jutted from the forest floor like knives. She could see perfectly by sun or moon. The world always looked the same to her.

Presently, she slowed her pace as she arrived at the designated rendezvous. She was hoping to be early. That way she could lie in wait—see what developed. Though she usually knew who her clients were, she didn't know this one. That in itself warranted caution. But it was not to be. Her mysterious client was already there.

Xiao-Hong morphed out of her demon-fox form as she approached.

"Did you get it?" the shadowy figure asked. It was a distorted man's voice. Xiao-Hong could not see his face. A bell-shaped straw hat covered his entire head, much like the kind wandering Komuso Buddhist monks and ninja assassins wore to conceal their identities. Only his eyes could be seen through the slits cut into the cap. They glowed with an eerie demonic fire.

"No," Xiao-Hong said apologetically. "I couldn't get a strand of her hair—but I did get this," she continued, producing Meilin's *iPod nano* from her robe's inner pocket.

The shadowy figure held out his hand, causing the miniature MP3 player to fly through the air from the Huli-jing's grasp. "This isn't what you were hired for," he said.

"But it's from her time. It was all I could do."

The shadow man closed his hand around the *iPod nano* as he considered its worth.

"You never said why you needed it," the demon fox remarked.

The shadow man didn't answer. Instead, he produced a small coin bag and tossed it to the ground behind the Huli-jing.

Xiao-Hong studied her client for a moment and she didn't like what she saw—a coldness even darker than hers. But a demon-fox had to work. The war was over. The Heavenly Court no longer required her services. She could go back to making a living by doing what Huli-jings did best—preying on the souls of foolish men—or make her living by stealth. She chose stealth.

As she turned her back on the shadow man to retrieve her payment, a sudden searing pain screamed through her body as her robes erupted into blue flame.

She felt the shadow man's hot breath on her neck. "Since when do Huli-jings ask questions!"

Xiao-Hong struggled to stagger forward as the fire enveloped and consumed her. Within the incomprehensible agony of the blazing inferno, she willed herself into her spirit fox-form as she fell to the leafy forest floor.

Her eyes stared blankly at the bamboo trees that surrounded her as she struggled to breathe.

After a few moments—her world went dark.

Chapter 3

Meilin and Jessie wove their way up the stairs amid the mass of students arriving at Midland Hills High. It was a sunny Monday morning but the air was cool, much cooler than normal for a typical southern California December day. But the temperature didn't seem to bother Jessie, who was preoccupied with the tune blaring from her magenta *iPod nano*.

"You gotta hear this!" Jessie said, plucking one of her tiny headset plugs from her ear and stretching it in Meilin's direction.

Meilin tilted her head closer to Jessie while they walked down the hallway toward their lockers.

"You got the new *Lady Ga Ga?*" Meilin gasped as Jessie tilted the *iPod nano's* tiny screen toward her so she could see the cover video.

"Downloaded it before breakfast—and the new *Taylor Swift* and *Black-eyed Peas!*"

"No way!"

"Yes, way!" Jessie reaffirmed. "Soon as they hit the e-store—bang—right into my account!"

"You're so lucky!" Meilin said. "There's no way my mom will ever let me buy anything online."

"Chillax girl! I got your back!" Jessie said, attempting to sound streetwise. It was a poor attempt at best, but that didn't stop her from trying. "Why do you think I got us matching nanos for your birthday? So we can share! I can't let my BFF go around tuneless—or clueless." Then Jessie smiled. "Hey—tuneless, clueless—they rhyme! Tuneless—clueless."

"You're a regular poet," Meilin said, rolling her eyes. Whatever "cool" Jessie might have garnered just went out the window as her usual geekiness resurfaced.

"So?" Jessie said, as the two girls continued to negotiate the crowded hallway.

"So?" Meilin repeated, not catching Jessie's drift.

"Give me your nano, silly," Jessie said restating the obvious. "I'll make the transfer at home tonight and give it back to you tomorrow."

"Duh..." Meilin grunted, slipping her backpack off her shoulder and zipping it open. After a few moments of hunting, "It's not here..." she said with both concern and confusion. "I had it yesterday—Oh snap! It must have fallen out of my bag at Master Zhang's!"

"You sure?" Jessie asked as Meilin rummaged through her backpack again.

"Dang, I'm sorry, Jess!" Meilin grunted again. "Uncle Z's really gonna be ticked that I left something behind."

"No biggie," Jessie remarked. She then added in a quieter tone, "You just go back through the *you-know-what* and get it. I mean, it's not like it's the end of the world, right?"

"I don't know. Uncle Z was really adamant about stuff like that when he laid out the rules for me using the..." Meilin paused, glanced around, lowered her voice and then whispered, "...*the you-know-what*."

"What you-know-what?" Jessie said loudly with a grin.

"Very funny," Meilin smirked. "Why don't you just blab everything over the P-A?"

"What?" Jessie repeated again, still enjoying her joke. But Meilin wasn't smiling.

"Look, there's nothing to worry about. I'll prove it." Jessie said.

Jessie quickly scanned the hallway.

"Oh, Aah-ron..." she called, summoning the nearby lanky freshman unloading his books into his locker.

The boy looked around, searching to see who called his name. He was surprised when he saw it was a girl, let alone Jessie with Meilin. He gave them a *Who me?* look.

"Yes, you!" Jessie waved. "C'mere."

"What are you doing?" Meilin whispered out of the side of her mouth.

"Proving my point and to do that, we need a nerd," Jesse whispered back, as Aaron clumsily made his way toward them through the bustling students.

"Be nice," Meilin said, feeling some empathy for the boy. Aaron was definitely on the strange side, a classic game card-carrying, action figure-collecting nerd, but he was smart.

"I'm always nice," Jessie rebutted with a smiling whisper. "Do you wanna tell him his barn door is open, or should I?"

"Eww!" both girls said in unison.

"You called me?" Aaron said when he finally reached the two girls. It was plain that he was extremely uncomfortable talking to them.

"Hypothetical question, Aaron," Jesse stated. "Someone from the present goes back in time, has a little fun, returns, but accidentally leaves something behind. No biggie, right?"

"No," Aaron replied firmly. "That'd be totally bad. It could alter the whole space-time continuum."

"See? Like I said, no problem." Jesse said with vindication—then did a double take. "Nerd-boy says what?"

"Sure. Like there's this movie where these future guys ran a safari service and they'd send high-roller clients back to prehistoric times, but one of them like shot this tree-monkey thing then got scared when a bunch of others came, so he dropped his gun and ran away. When he got back to the future, like everything was different and these weird monkey-things evolved and he was like the only human left...and stuff? Really cool film. I watched it five times."

"Y-e-a-h..." Jessie drawled slowly. "Thanks Aaron. You can go now."

Aaron's head bobbed up and down as he nodded, but didn't move.

"Aaron..." Jessie said again as she made a shooing gesture with her hand.

"Oh, sorry," Aaron said as he finally got the drift that he was dismissed.

"Thanks, Aaron," Meilin called as he awkwardly walked back to his locker, bumping into several students as he did so.

"So I picked the wrong nerd," Jesse complained. "Big deal! It's not like someone's gonna discover the Jade Emperor's tomb and find a flat-screen TV in it or something—and OMG—tell me I didn't just die and go to heaven!" Jesse said, suddenly changing the subject.

Meilin turned and looked in the direction Jesse was staring. Walking down the hall was a boy—a really good-looking boy. Tall, dark red hair, ruddy complexion, athletic build, chiseled magazine-model face. His aura projected an air of mystery mixed with a hint of *bad boy*—and he appeared to be walking straight for them.

Meilin's whole body began to tingle. Her monkey-senses went on full alert. Why?

Tiffany!

"Connor! There you are!" Meilin heard Tiffany gush as she and her posse intercepted the new boy twenty feet from where Meilin and Jessie were standing. "Your locker's this way. Let me show you."

Tiffany ushered the boy down the hall. He turned his head slightly in Meilin and Jessie's direction as he passed.

"Eee!" Jessie squealed, turning to her friend. "He looked at us! Tell me he looked at us!" she said grabbing Meilin's arm and dancing up and down. "Oh please-please-please let him be in one of my classes!"

"Whoa! Now *you* chillax!" Meilin laughed. "It's just a new kid. So what."

"So what!" Jessie spat. "Hello? Didn't you see him? He's freakin' hot!"

"Yeah-yeah," Meilin shrugged. "Like either of us would ever have a chance. You saw who scooped him up."

"Wow!" Jessie replied, surprised with Meilin's sudden dourness. "When did you jump on the grumpy bus?"

Jessie was right. Why did it matter to Meilin? Was it because she knew she'd never have a chance with a boy like that—or was it deeper? Maybe it was because she knew inside that she'd never have a chance with *any* boy at all. How could she? She was half-monkey for crying out loud. Who'd want to go out with a girl like *her!*

The two-minute homeroom-warning bell rang.

"Rats!" Jessie said. "See you at lunch!" she added as she trotted down the hall. The two girls' lockers were located, unfortunately, in opposite directions. They also didn't share any classes together except for gym and 5th period math. This blunder by the school's administration was further compounded by the fact that Meilin's nemesis, Tiffany Edwards, shared nearly all of Meilin's classes. To further the insult, Meilin's locker was located two spaces down from Tiffany's. The school couldn't have devised a worse situation for her if they tried.

Meilin walked past Tiffany and her Tiffany-clone posse, ignoring their looks of smug disdain. Two months ago, this would have bothered Meilin and brought her to tears, like it did in middle school when Tiffany first began to demean her, calling her *chopstick* and making fun of her clothes.

Now, Meilin simply didn't care. *She* was the one perpetrating the façade of the timid and easily harassed girl. Tiffany's bullying was on *her* terms. Still, this didn't make Meilin feel any better about it. Tiffany had everything in this world—the California tan, blonde hair, the good looks and the money—and she used everything she had to her advantage, even if it meant stepping on everyone around her to get her way.

Meilin spun the padlock hanging on her locker door. She then gave it a tug. It didn't open. Did she dial the combination correctly? She tried again. 16-35-10, pull. Again the padlock didn't open.

Meilin heard giggles off to her side. It was Tiffany and her crew. They were up to something. She knew it! Meilin covertly evoked her demon monkey-enhanced vision and examined her lock. Her jaw muscles tightened as she discovered the problem—superglue!

"Having a little trouble, *chopstick*?" Tiffany asked, feigning concern.

Meilin's eyes narrowed as her anger began to well. This time Tiffany went too far. She had half a mind to...

"Need some help?" a voice suddenly interrupted.

Meilin turned her head. It was the new kid, Connor, standing right behind her. Meilin's anger instantly dissipated, replaced with the question of *Why didn't I sense you approach?*

"Let me try," he offered, reaching across Meilin, and taking her lock in his hands. "Sometimes you just have to give these things a good tug."

Connor tugged once on the frozen lock and it miraculously opened.

"There, see?" he said with a smile. It was a very nice smile and Meilin felt her heart skip a beat.

"Thanks," Meilin heard herself mutter. Connor acknowledged Meilin with a wink.

The final homeroom bell sounded.

"Connor! Hurry or you'll be late!" Tiffany said, stepping in and taking his arm. "Can't have that on your first day," she added as she nearly dragged the boy down the hall. Her posse fell in around their leader, further insuring that Connor couldn't *get away.*

"You know," Meilin heard Tiffany remark as they receded down the hallway, "if you wanna get the most out of your next four years here at MHH, there's certain people you'll want to associate with—and," Tiffany paused, turning her head ever so slightly back in Meilin's direction, "several you really need to avoid..."

Meilin's hand tightened around the padlock in her palm. Its steel shackle snapped in two from the pressure of her vice-like monkey-grip. Her eyes drifted down to the broken lock in her hand, not sure if she was mad at Tiffany's malicious prank—or at herself for allowing it to happen. Either way, she was out ten bucks for a new lock.

Chapter 4

"There he is!" Jessie said, nearly choking on her baloney sandwich as Connor came through the lunch line carrying his tray. "Scoot over," she added under her breath, motioning for Meilin to shift over one seat at their table with a slight nod of her head.

"That's a little obvious, don't ya think?" Meilin replied.

"Don't care! Just do it!" Then Jessie added with a softer tone, "Please."

Meilin stared at Jessie for a second, then complied, shifting her lunch over to the next chair across from her friend.

"You're completely nuts, ya know!" Meilin smiled.

"So?" Jessie returned. Her eyes lit up as Connor seemed to gravitate in their direction as he scanned the lunchroom looking for an empty seat.

"Connor!" a familiar voice called out. "Over here!"

Jessie's face dropped as Connor abruptly changed direction and headed for Tiffany's table.

"This is where the elite sit," she continued as Connor joined her. She then went on to introduce him to the other boys and girls at her table. "This is Carol. Samantha. That's Mackenzie. That's Marty Woods of Woods Hotel fame. Dennis Munroe, his father anchors the evening news..."

"Ah, poop!" Jessie griped, tossing the last quarter of her baloney sandwich on top of her brown paper lunch bag.

"C'mon," Meilin smirked. "You knew that was gonna happen."

"Yeah, but a girl can dream," Jessie replied.

"His name's Connor Hunt," Meilin stated. "He's fifteen. His father's in the military, that's why he's a transfer student. He's attended three different middle schools growing up, the last one in Germany, of all places."

Jessie's mouth dropped open with utter amazement.

"He's in my homeroom," Meilin said, removing the mystery of her apparent omniscience. "Mr. Schubert introduced him to the class."

"Anything else?" Jessie grunted.

"Yeah, he's sitting at Tiffany's table. So give it up."

"Yeah..." Jessie echoed with defeat as she picked up her milk carton. She sucked loudly on her straw, determined to drain every last milliliter of milk from the container.

Her eyes suddenly lit up again as she tossed the empty carton aside. "Ooo! I forgot to tell you— I signed us up for a new sport. And in this one, you don't have to hold back."

"New sport?" Meilin said. "What new sport?"

"Gymnastics, silly!"

"You *are* crazy!" Meilin said.

"C'mon, you're a natural. Especially with your..."

"Skills?"

"Look, volleyball's over and soccer doesn't start 'til spring. You could take the school straight to State championship without breaking a sweat— which—is exactly why you can't do it," Jessie frowned, processing the full logic of the scenario for herself in her head. "Sorry," she shrugged. "Guess I wasn't thinking. I just feel like doing something physical and it was either that or cheerleading."

Both girls looked at each other. "*Eww!*"

Meilin stared at her friend for another moment then said reluctantly, "Okay, let's do it."

Jessie's face lit up. "You mean it?"

"Sure," Meilin replied. "Sounds like fun. Besides, it's definitely something where I wouldn't have to worry about Miss Perfect. I don't think she'd know a balance beam from a two-by-four if one fell on her foot."

"Ooo... Testy! Something happen?"

"She superglued my lock shut."

Jessie cracked a grin. "Well, you gotta admit, that's a good one!"

Meilin reached into her pocket and placed the pieces of her padlock on the table.

"Remind me to never make you mad," Jessie remarked, staring at the broken shackle.

"Yeah, well, I did this after it was already opened," Meilin said.

Jessie shot her a quizzical look.

"I was gonna open it. But Connor appeared outta nowhere and opened it for me."

"Awesome! He did? Dang! Why couldn't Tiffany glue *my* lock shut." Jessie said, her eyes lighting up again. "You have all the luck!"

"Ya think?" Meilin remarked, dismissively. "I'm just wondering how he did it. It was glued solid."

"Was it?" Jessie returned. "I hate to tell ya, but you've been riding the Bummerville Express for a couple of weeks now—ever since you started your training back in... you know where. Are you sure you weren't so focused on Tiffany that maybe your lock wasn't glued as tight as you thought?"

Jessie was right. Meilin was feeling off center—about almost everything.

"Maybe," Meilin reluctantly admitted. "Sorry I've been no fun lately. It's just that..."

"Look, we all have bad days," Jessie said, cutting Meilin off. "Maybe you should talk to your mom or your Uncle Z. I'm sure he's got one of those fortune cookie sayings of his that covers whatever's bothering you."

"Probably," Meilin nodded. Then she smiled. "Fortune cookie sayings—he'll like that."

"You know what I mean."

Indeed, Meilin *did* know what Jessie meant. Over five thousand years of ancient wisdom had been reduced to little more than fortune cookie sayings in this day and age of fast food, instant messages, and instant gratification. It was no wonder Meilin felt off balance. Yet the world she was born in was out of balance, too. Maybe, no matter where or when a person lived, there was always something out of balance.

The period bell rang. Lunch was over.

Chapter 5

Meilin sat alone at a corner workbench near a rear window in the high school's Chemistry Lab. Chemistry was a required course and not one Meilin would have normally elected if she had a choice. But it came easy to her, no doubt because she was exceptional at math. "Everything in the universe," her eighth grade math teacher once proclaimed, "could ultimately be reduced to some form of mathematics." Meilin wasn't sure if that was true, but then again, mathematicians were a weird lot. Everything was a number to them, a plus, a minus, a one or a zero. A positive. A negative. A Yin. A Yang. "Hmm," Meilin pondered, letting her mind wander. Was there math in the Tao? Could the Tao be reduced to a math equation? Now, *this* was something worth thinking about. Would Uncle Z have a saying about this? This was definitely something she'd put to him later. But, right now, her teacher, Mr. Petrush, was droning on about sodium.

"Sodium," Mr. Petrush stated with the earnest passion of one who truly loved his subject, even if said passion was totally lost on the many blank faces in his class, "this white stuff that we all know as one of the elements of common table salt, is in fact, a metal. —*What?* A metal you say?" the thin man of 30 added, trying to make his lecture sound interesting. His eyes sparkled behind the lab glasses that he always wore. "Why yes, indeed! A metal. And it has some amazing properties which..."

The door to the lab opened, interrupting Mr. Petrush's lecture. A boy walked in, carrying a note. It was Connor Hunt.

Mr. Petrush looked at the note and nodded.

"Mr. Hunt is joining our class," he announced. Immediately, all the girls stirred in their chairs. Then to Connor, "Grab an empty seat," he said as he handed the teen a pair of safety goggles from the box on his desk.

"And one more thing," Mr. Petrush added, gesturing towards his own ear. "Lose the earplugs."

"Oh, sorry," Connor replied, pulling the mini earplugs from his ears and shoving the wires into his shirt pocket. "Sometimes I forget."

Mr. Petrush nodded and pointed a finger, indicating that Connor should hurry and find a place.

Connor scanned the room. Tiffany waved at him. The seat next to her was empty. He nodded and gravitated her way. As he neared, the beaker of water on the workbench in front of Tiffany somehow suddenly tipped over. The clear liquid ran across the tabletop and rained down across the empty seat, soaking it.

Connor made an *oops* face as he walked past the dripping chair, finally settling, of all places, next to Meilin, leaving Tiffany beside herself with a *how the heck did that happen* expression on her face, as well as a flooded tabletop.

"You mind?" he asked Meilin with a whisper, before sitting.

"Um... no," Meilin said with a hint of surprise in her voice. She slid her books aside, making room for him. Tiffany didn't have a partner at her table because she wanted the whole station to herself. Meilin didn't have a partner because no one wanted to sit with her.

"Cool," Connor replied, taking his place next to her.

Meilin could feel Tiffany glaring at her from across the room. "Aren't you afraid you'll..." Meilin said, motioning slightly toward Tiffany.

"Wreck my rep by sitting at the wrong table?" Connor interrupted with a smile.

Meilin shrugged a *well, yeah.*

"I'll take my chances," he grinned. "Besides, I heard you're pretty smart. I'll need a good lab partner to pass this class."

Meilin shrugged at the compliment.

"And I'm a little bit tired of people trying to choose my friends for me. I get enough of that at home."

"If we're all settled?" Mr. Petrush said with some annoyance. The interruption definitely threw his presentation off pace. Then to Tiffany, "Miss Edwards?"

"I swear I didn't touch a thing." she replied, still sopping up the mess with several paper towels.

"Yes, well... when you're done, please refill your beaker half way with water so we can continue."

The exasperated teen hurriedly mopped up the water and refilled her beaker.

"Right," Mr. Petrush then said. "Sodium, as I said, is a low elemental metal, with some remarkable properties. When placed in water, it turns the solution alkaline, releasing hydrogen in the process. And because it has a low boiling point of 96 degrees—voila!" he concluded, dropping the small piece of sodium he gripped with his long lab tweezers into the demonstration beaker on his desk. It immediately fizzed, floated to the top then suddenly erupted into a flaming ball of orange fire with a loud snapping sound.

"Now that's what I call *real* firewater!" Mr. Petrush concluded with a satisfied grin.

The demonstration certainly brought the class to attention, especially the boys who burst out with "cool!" and "awesome!"

"Naturally, this is something you absolutely *never* try at home," Mr. Petrush stated strongly. "But here in the lab, we'll give it a go. So, glasses on, everyone! In the small vial at each workstation, you'll find a small nugget of sodium submersed in oil. That's to keep it from oxidizing in the air. Take it out with your lab tweezers and pop it into your beakers of water. Don't put your cheery faces near the beakers if you value your eyebrows."

Meilin looked at Connor, giving him a *go ahead, you do it* nod.

Connor nodded in return and picked up the small glass vial containing their tiny nugget of sodium. He spun the cap off with his thumb and withdrew the nugget with his lab tweezers.

"Ready?" he said before dropping the sodium nugget into the water.

Meilin nodded, leaning away in her chair. All around her, the class was tittering with excitement as their beakers popped, fizzed and boiled with fire.

"Here goes," Connor said, dropping their nugget of sodium into the beaker.

The sodium nugget fell into the water with a tiny plop and sank to the bottom. It then started to fizz and float to the top. When the nugget broke to the surface in the beaker, it erupted into flame. But not like the flame in the other students' experiments. This flame was bright blue and shot up several feet into the air. The flame was blazingly hot, so hot that the beaker itself exploded with a loud bang, showering Meilin and Connor with flying glass.

Meilin's reaction was instinctive. Moving at lightning speed, she shielded herself with her notebook. Connor was not so lucky or as fast. Several needle-like shards of glass peppered his forearm that he fortunately managed to cover his face with.

"Oh my God!" Mr. Petrush cried as he raced to their workstation. The blue flame still shot to the ceiling—right off the stone tabletop. Then abruptly, it ceased.

"Are you two all right?" he demanded.

"I'm fine," Meilin said, her voice shaking.

"I..." Connor grimaced. His forearm was bleeding where the many shards of glass pierced his skin.

"Nurse, immediately!" Mr. Petrush ordered, placing a hand under Connor's upper arm and standing him up.

"Meilin?" he asked again with concern.

"I'm okay," Meilin reiterated. She was. Her innate demon monkey reflexes saved her from a face full of glass. Her notebook didn't fare as well, as evidenced by the shard-riddled rear cover.

"You had water in that beaker, right?" Mr. Petrush questioned.

"From the tap!" Meilin replied. Meilin could see from her teacher's expression that what just occurred was chemically impossible.

"Look, I'm okay," Connor insisted. "It's just a couple'a scratches."

"Sorry, school policy," Mr. Petrush returned. "Let's go!" he ordered, guiding Connor along with him.

"Everyone clean up your stations and sit tight 'till I get back," Mr. Petrush said as he opened the door to the lab. And then he and Connor were gone.

The door barely shut before Tiffany was on her feet.

"Nice going, *chopstick*!" Tiffany lashed out. "You almost blew us all up!"

"I didn't do anything!" Meilin stammered in her own defense, still unsure of what just happened. There was only water in her beaker—she was certain of that. And the nugget of sodium in her vial was the same, if not smaller than the ones her classmates had. What had happened was impossible—yet the shattered glass beaker was evidence to the contrary.

Meilin grit her teeth as Tiffany rambled on. "You're just lucky Connor wasn't killed!"

Tiffany was right about that. It was lucky that Connor, or any one else sitting nearby, wasn't seriously hurt. "You're dangerous—that's what you are! *Dangerous!*"

Meilin's eyes welled up—not at what Tiffany said, but because of the look on the faces of her fellow classmates. It was very plain that they all agreed.

Chapter 6

U ncle Z listened with great concern as Meilin recited the day's events. Tears rolled down her face as she concluded her story with the strange explosion that injured Connor.

"The whole class hates me and thinks it's my fault," Meilin said.

"Was it?" Zhu Bajie asked. He shifted his tremendous weight on the couch he and Meilin were sitting on in the rear of his *Heavenly River Imports* antique shop.

"No," Meilin sniffled.

Zhu Bajie put his massive arm around Meilin's shoulders and drew her close. "Let me tell you something my old friend Lao Tzu once said: *'Care about what other people think and you'll always be their prisoner.'*"

Meilin tried to smile. "When did he say that?"

"At one of the Jade Emperor's birthday banquets. They brought out this giant juicy roast and being the pig that I am," he chuckled, remembering the savory event, "naturally I wanted the whole thing for myself. But if I ate it, then everyone at the table would be mad. It was a real dilemma."

"So what did you do?" she said, wiping her eyes dry with her hand.

"I ate the whole darn thing! And the next two they brought out as well!" Zhu Bajie stated as Meilin's expression changed from a frown to a smile. "After all, I *am* a pig, right? Of course, old Lao was ticked because he didn't get any, but it was his own fault for bestowing his *wisdom* on me."

Zhu Bajie then became a bit more serious. "Look, your mom and I know that leading a double life is hard for you. There's gonna be many days like this, not only in school, but in the other aspects of your life. But the one thing you can always rely on is that we'll always be here for you. Same goes for your father. You're not alone, Meilin. Don't ever think you are. The main thing you have to remember is always to be true to your inner Tao. If you can do that, you'll always be in harmony with yourself and the world."

"But it's hard!" Meilin said. "Sometimes I feel like I just don't belong—anywhere! I'm just a kid, Uncle Z."

"I know," Zhu Bajie replied. "Sometimes I feel the same way. Heck, I used to be the Heavenly Commander of the Celestial Navy. Now I'm a big fat demon pig running an antique shop in downtown Midland Hills! Who'd ever figure *that* would happen? But you gotta face things head on. *'There are only two mistakes one can make along the road in life: One, not going all the way; and two, not starting.'*"

"Another one of Lao Tzu's sayings?" Meilin smiled.

"Nope," Zhu Bajie replied. "Buddha told me that one. The point is, you take it one step at a time, embracing everything life throws at you."

"And if life deals you lemons—make lemonade," Meilin interjected.

"There you go!" Zhu Bajie smiled. "Not that I would put it that way, but yeah."

Meilin gave her uncle a hug. "Thanks Uncle Z," she said. Then she laughed. "Jessie said you'd have the right 'fortune cookie' saying to make me feel better."

"Ha!" Zhu Bajie snorted. "Don't get me started on fortune cookies! I came up with that idea several thousand years ago. A great way to market all those enigmatic wisdoms Lao was always spouting. But was the stuffy old fart interested? Noooo! It wasn't *sagely*. Too bad. We could'a made a fortune together. Get it? Fortune? Fortune-cookie?" Zhu Bajie finished with a laugh.

"Yeah," Meilin grunted. "I got it. You and Jessie should team up. You're both regular comedians."

"Who's a comedian?" Meilin's mother asked, as she reached the top of the stairs that led from her Chinese herbal apothecary located in the lower level of Zhu Bajie's shop. The apothecary was in fact the only part of the business that generated any real income. Zhu Bajie rarely sold any antiques, mostly because he hated to part with anything he collected. It was Lijuan's reputation throughout the Asian community as a healer that kept the family afloat. Even though she only charged her clients the cost of the herbs and other ingredients she used in the preparation of her remedies, many insisted on paying her more. For those who could not afford to pay anything, her potions and concoctions were free.

Lijuan was dressed in a traditional Chinese red *qipao*—the color red having the power to bring good luck, but also the power to dispel ghosts. Her long, black hair flowed down to the small of her back, further accentuating her exotic beauty. Meilin secretly hoped that she would grow up to be as pretty—but then, nearly all Chinese fairy folk were blessed this way. Meilin was only half-fairy. The other half was demon monkey, so she wasn't so sure.

"Uncle Z," Meilin answered with a wink to her uncle, "trying to be *punny* again."

Zhu Bajie smiled, "Ah, good one."

"Hmph," Lijuan remarked as she joined them. "Anything I should know about?" she asked.

"No," Zhu Bajie replied. "Just having a little chat about life in general. Nothing big."

Lijuan smiled. She was grateful that Meilin was comfortable enough to talk over her problems with her uncle. Zhu Bajie was like a second father to her, especially in the absence of her real father, Sun Wukong, whom she was just getting to know.

"Well, what say we close early and get some dinner?" Lijuan said.

"Now, that's the best idea I've heard all day!" Zhu Bajie replied, standing. "I'm thinking a roast—a couple of roasts!" he said with a grin.

Meilin was about to agree when the ancient Gate—the magical portal to the past that stood a few feet from the couch she was sitting on in the rear of the shop, began to rattle. A thin vertical line of blinding blue light emanated from the seam where the two wooden doors joined.

Instantly Zhu Bajie morphed into his true

demon form—that of Pigsy the Pig. His nine-toothed rake of pure ice-metal materialized in his hands.

"Stand back!" he ordered. "Someone wants to come through!"

"But no one can come through without the keys," Meilin said, taking a protective fighting stance in front of her mother. Lijuan was a healer, not a warrior, and after what happened the last time when Bull King's demon forces managed to come through the Gate and capture her mother, Zhu Bajie and Meilin took no chances. But that only happened because Meilin had placed the three magical keys into the lock. The Gate was supposed to have been inactive, but as it turned out—it wasn't. It was that fateful event on her fourteenth birthday that propelled Meilin down the path to discovering who she truly was.

Meilin looked at her uncle. "What should we do?"

Zhu Bajie thought a moment then said, "Open it!"

Meilin hesitated, but then withdrew the three jade hair sticks from her ponytail knot. With a flick of her wrist, she willed them to fly into the three holes atop the ancient rusted lock.

Instantly the lock opened.

As the doors began to part, the three jade hair sticks flew back into her hand. Meilin poked the two smaller ones back into her ponytail knot. The longer of the set morphed into her bo-sized jade fighting staff. Even though the Gate was located within the protected safety of Shuilian-dong, they would take no chances.

Within moments, a lone demon monkey stepped through the vortex. Meilin recognized him as one of the spiritual shamans from Shuilian-dong. He was momentarily disoriented, but the sensation of traveling through time quickly dissipated. He went down on one knee, after recognizing Meilin and Lijuan.

Your Highnesses," he said, staring at the floor. "Forgive the intrusion, but the elders thought it urgent. A Huli-jing was found nearly burned to death in the forest. Sha Wujing had her brought to us. My Queen," he said to Lijuan, "we need you."

"Of course," Lijuan replied. "I'll come immediately."

"There's one more thing," the monkey shaman said, still kneeling. "The Huli-jing managed to utter only one word..." The demon monkey then lifted his head and looked directly at Meilin. "She said *your* name, Princess. She said—*Meilin*."

Chapter 7

"I'm going, too!" Meilin announced as her mind raced. Could it be? She only knew one Huli-jing—Xiao-Hong. Was it her? If it was, what on earth could have happened?

"No!" Lijuan said firmly.

"But, Mom..." Meilin protested.

"Your mother's right," Zhu Bajie said, reinforcing Lijuan's command. "Until we know what happened, it's best you remain here. Besides, you have school."

"But Xiao-Hong said my name," Meilin countered.

"Xiao-Hong?" Zhu Bajie said with sudden concern.

"Well," Meilin replied with hesitation. "I only know one Huli-jing—and she was at my last training session with Master Zhang."

"That definitely seals it!" Lijuan said. "You're

staying here!"

"But Mom—she was nice—sort of."

"What have we warned you about Huli-jings?" Lijuan demanded.

"That they can't be trusted," Meilin uttered.

"And why?"

"Because they have no soul," Meilin said.

"That's right! They don't! That's their nature."

"But Mom, Xiao-Hong isn't evil, I know it!"

"Meilin!" Zhu Bajie stated firmly.

Meilin knew well enough not to pursue the matter further. The issue was closed, especially with her uncle siding with her mother.

Lijuan quickly gathered a canvas tote bag full of medicinal herbs from her massive inventory in her downstairs apothecary. Though much of what she needed could undoubtedly be found and gathered from the lush forests of the Huaguo Mountains, Lijuan didn't want to risk any delay in treatment. She didn't know what to expect or what she could do for the Huli-jing—burn victims required all of her healing skill, and still there was no guarantee of success.

Lijuan also didn't have to remind Zhu Bajie to mind the fort and take care of Meilin while she was away. Zhu Bajie took his responsibility of caring for and protecting Meilin extremely seriously. It was an oath he swore to Meilin's father, Sun Wukong, thousands of years ago, just before he stepped through the Gate that transported the infant Meilin and her mother forward in time—safe from Bull King's clutches, or so they thought.

Lijuan hugged Meilin before stepping through the Gate's magical vortex. "Don't give your uncle a hard time and make sure you get your homework done."

"Mom!" Meilin complained. "I'm not a kid anymore."

"And go to bed early!" Lijuan added.

"Mom..." Meilin repeated, rolling her eyes.

"Don't worry about us," Zhu Bajie stated. "We'll be fine."

Lijuan nodded as she hefted her tote bag onto her shoulder. Immediately, the shaman monk stood and stepped forward, wanting to carry Lijuan's bag for her. But Lijuan waved him off by gesturing toward the Gate. Lijuan was his Queen, but would neither demand nor accept any special treatment. She would not suffer anyone bearing any burden she would not bear herself—even something so simple as carrying her own bag.

When Lijuan was among the demon monkeys at Shuilian-dong, she did exactly as they did— gathered fruit, washed clothes in the streams, saw to the needs of the elderly and most especially—saw to the needs of the children. Meilin was always amazed at how giving her mother could be and how relaxed she was with everyone she encountered. She was of the fairy-folk—very different from those of monkey-kind. But this seemed to have no bearing on her attitude or personality. Perhaps this is what attracted her father to her.

Meilin prayed that she would one day be as accepting and giving as her mother. But in order to do that, she knew that she had to conquer her inner fears and self-doubt. If she couldn't, then she would always be out of balance with her Tao.

Meilin waved to her mother as she and the monkey shaman stepped into the Gate's magical vortex and disappeared. The vortex then vanished and the ancient wooden doors slammed shut of their own accord. The rusted lock clicked securely in place, sealing the gateway to the past. No one except her father or her grandmother could open the Gate without the keys—and this was only because their combined magic created it. Magic directed at the Gate by others could rattle the doors. But without the keys to open the lock, the doors would never part. This meant that conceivably Meilin's mother could never return from the past unless Meilin opened the gate for her from this end.

"Well, I think we were talking about dinner. A couple of juicy roasts, if I'm not mistaken," Zhu Bajie said, as he morphed back into his human form. His nine-tooth rake morphed into a metallic comb that the 300-pound man ran through his bristly black hair. Satisfied with his mop, his comb then vanished.

"Uncle Z..." Meilin said, shaking her head with amusement.

"What? A pig's gotta eat!" he rebutted.

Meilin shrugged. There was no arguing with a pig—especially a demon pig.

"Hit the lights," Zhu Bajie said as he flipped the OPEN sign to CLOSED on the shop's front door.

As the two walked toward Zhu Bajie's trusty but rusty minivan parked in the rear of the shop, Zhu Bajie paused and looked down at his niece. "That fire," he said. "You said it was—blue?"

"Yeah," Meilin nodded.

"And everyone else's was yellowy orange."

Meilin nodded again.

Zhu Bajie resumed walking. "And it danced on water, even after your beaker exploded..."

"Kind'a. Why?"

Zhu Bajie shrugged and didn't answer.

Chapter 8

When Meilin arrived at school the next day, she got the cold shoulder from nearly everyone in the hallway. Tiffany and her posse had already spread the word about what had happened in the Chemistry Lab the previous afternoon, embellishing the story enough to make Meilin responsible for the mishap that, in Tiffany's words, *"almost killed"* Connor.

"Don't even pay attention to them!" Jessie advised her friend.

"Yeah," Meilin said glumly as they moved through the throng of students, their silent stares accusing her. She was already feeling bad enough about what occurred in the lab—she didn't need this piled on top of everything else that happened.

Her mother being suddenly summoned to Shuilian-Dong didn't sit well with her either. The burned Huli-jing that was found must really be in critical condition for the Elders of the Monkey Kingdom to expend their collective magic in order to summon her mother across time. Meilin prayed it wasn't Xiao-Hong. But who else could it be?

Meilin's eyes scanned the hall as the two walked. She was anxious to locate Connor—see if he was all right—even apologize to him, though she knew she didn't do anything wrong. Still, what happened couldn't be explained, no matter how many times she went over it during her sleepless night. Maybe it *was* her fault. Maybe she *did* do something wrong. But there was only water in her beaker—she was certain of that.

"Well, see ya later," Jessie said with a wave as the two reached the intersection that led to their respective lockers.

Meilin nodded as Jessie turned down the hallway. She then spun on her heel and walked in the opposite direction toward her own locker.

Meilin paused a moment, her eyes lighting up. She saw Connor, standing at his locker at the far end of the hall. Meilin's spirits rose. "He must be okay," she thought. "Otherwise, he would have stayed home."

Then, as the students in the distance thinned, Meilin's spirits fell. Tiffany! She was with Connor—almost clinging to him. How could she talk to him with *her* there!

It was a question that would go unanswered as three girls from Tiffany's posse stepped in front of Meilin, blocking her path.

"That's close enough, *chopstick!*" the taller girl in the clique said firmly. It was Mackenzie, one of Tiffany's inner circle.

"*Chopstick?*" Meilin repeated, surprised at the slur. Only Tiffany dared call her that—and even then, cautiously, especially after Meilin creamed her on the volleyball court when she returned from her adventure of self-discovery a few months ago. Meilin never could figure out why Tiffany hated her so much, even back then. For the other girls in her posse to call Meilin *chopstick* was a departure in their behavior. Was the clique getting bolder? If they were...

"You stay away from Connor. Far away!" said the other Tiffany clone, Samantha.

"You're kidding, right?" Meilin replied.

"Do we look like we're kidding?" the third Tiffany clone remarked.

"My locker's down there." Meilin objected.

"Not any more," Mackenzie said, as she lifted the top off the nearby hallway trash bin and dropped it on the floor. "This is your locker now."

Meilin's eyes widened. The bin was filled with the entire contents of her locker—her books, her photos, her papers—everything.

"Get the message?" Mackenzie said.

"We're tired of you!" Samantha stated flatly.

"The whole school's tired of you," Mackenzie reiterated.

The girls didn't wait for Meilin to respond. They turned their backs on her and walked away, joined Tiffany and Connor and headed off to class.

Meilin's eyes narrowed as her mind raced. What was going on? Tiffany's posse never behaved this way before. They were into make-up, fashion, and kowtowing to their leader, not overt physical threats. This wasn't like Tiffany, either. Tiffany was deceitful and devious. She'd never do something so blatantly malicious, especially not in public.

Meilin suppressed her anger and began extracting the contents of her locker from the trash bin. Retaliation on her part would solve nothing and put her further out of balance with her Tao. *"Whether big or small, many or few, return hatred with virtue,"* Uncle Zhu would say. Of course he'd say that after clobbering them with his nine-toothed rake. But Tiffany and her clique weren't demons, even if they acted like them.

Chapter 9

"**D**on't tell me you're going to let them get away with it!" Jessie fumed. Her face was as red with anger as the gym jersey she was wearing. Both girls stood near the end of a line of ten girls in the corner of the gym waiting to try out for gymnastics.

"Basically, yeah," Meilin replied with a hushed voice. "What else can I do? Go monkey on them?"

"I would!" Jessie growled. "I'd kung fu them right into next week!"

Meilin eyed her friend.

"Okay-okay—so you can't do that, but c'mon, Meilin," Jessie implored. "You can't roll over on everything for the next four years. If you do, I mean, how will you survive? How will you even respect yourself?"

Jessie had a point. How *would* Meilin respect herself if she did nothing?

"If you told me this at lunch, I'd have gone right over to their table and..."

"And what? Dumped your beanie-weenies on Tiffany's head?"

"Since I don't like beanie-weenies—yeah!"

"Right, then *you'd* be the one with detention. Besides, you were too busy gawking at Connor across the room."

"Oh, yeah. Connor," Jessie said dreamily. "Did you get to talk to him?"

"No," Meilin sighed. "He wasn't in any of my classes today."

"Girls?" Coach Daniels interrupted. "Are you joining us or are you dressed up for fun?"

"Sorry, Miss Daniels," Meilin smiled. They hadn't noticed that the line of girls had long since moved on and it was their turn.

"We're here to try out for the team," Jessie said, taking Meilin's arm and ushering her reluctant friend over. Even though Meilin said she'd sign up for the team with Jessie, she was already having second thoughts.

"This be the place," Coach Daniels said, checking their names off her list. At 24 years old, Coach Daniels was the youngest and newest Phys-Ed teacher at Midland Hills High. She was also the most liked. In addition to being the volleyball coach, she was also the girls' gymnastics coach.

"How's your leg?" Coach Daniels asked Meilin.

"Better, thanks," Meilin replied, remembering that it was a feigned pulled muscle that sidelined her from volleyball.

"Did you bring your signed permission slips?" Coach Daniels asked.

"Permission slips?" Jessie stated blankly. "Oh snap!"

Coach Daniels shook her head slightly. She then slipped two blank permission slips out from the bottom of her clipboard and handed them to the girls.

"Have your parents sign these and bring them back to me tomorrow."

Jessie frowned. "Does this mean we can't try out today?"

"Well, technically you're not supposed to," Coach Daniels said, "but I'll make an exception just for today since I have waivers on file for volleyball. But these have to be completed and returned before any serious training can begin."

Both girls nodded.

"Okay. Can either of you do a cartwheel?" Coach Daniels asked.

"Sure," Jessie answered. Meilin nodded in agreement.

"Well?" the coach said, gesturing with her hand for the girls to proceed.

"Oh," Jessie said. "You mean do one now?"

"That would be the general idea."

Jessie looked at Meilin and shrugged. They turned in unison, took a step and did their cartwheels. Jessie's was a tad lopsided. Meilin's was perfect.

"Very nice," Coach Daniels noted. "How about a handstand?"

Both girls nodded again. They then stepped forward, bent at the waist, placed both hands flat on the ground, kicked up their legs and went into handstands.

"Just like in the backyard," Jessie remarked as she strained to hold her position.

"Except for the rocks," Meilin agreed, remembering the fun the two of them had doing handstands, cartwheels and hanging upside down on Jessie's backyard swing set during the many summers they played together growing up.

"And dog poop," Jessie added, referring to the many unwanted surprises Cookie, her tiny Pomeranian, would leave around the backyard. It was Jessie's little brother's job to clean up after Cookie—a job he often conveniently "forgot" to do.

Coach Daniels studied the two girls. She could see Jessie struggling hard to maintain the position, but Meilin wasn't. She was perfectly relaxed, as if the handstand was effortless.

"That's pretty good," Coach Daniels said, signaling Jessie and Meilin to return to a standing position.

"Either of you know what a walkover is?"

Both girls shook their heads, no.

"That's when you take a step forward or backward, kick up into a handstand, continue the motion through and return to a standing position."

"Oh, that! That's easy," Jessie said. "How about something harder like one of those handsprings to a somersault things?"

"A full-out? You girls can do that?" Coach Daniels said suspiciously.

"Well, not me, but Meilin can. She can do all that fancy stuff. Front flips. Back flips. Side flips," Jessie stated boldly.

"What are you doing!" Meilin whispered out of the corner of her mouth as she pulled Jessie around while pretending to cough.

"Getting you a good spot on the team," Jessie replied. She smiled as she turned back to Coach Daniels. "We have a trampoline in our backyard," she said, stretching the truth. She did have something like a trampoline, of sorts—a miniature one her mother used for her aerobic workouts. "Meilin can do all of those fancy moves."

"Oh, a trampoline," Coach Daniels remarked, as if that impressed her. "Well, that's certainly an element of the sport, but unfortunately not here. The school can't cover the liability. We're working strictly on floor-ex, vaulting, balance beam and the uneven bars. Are any of these of interest to you?"

"Sure," Jessie answered. "We'll do them all!"

Coach Daniels smiled. "How about we just start with the basics and work our way up—see what fits best."

"Okay," Jessie said. "But Meilin really can do everything. You should probably start her out at the top," Jessie bragged. "The girl's a natural."

"Really? I didn't know we had an Olympian right under our noses," Coach Daniels smiled.

"Well," Meilin protested. "I wouldn't exactly say that..."

"She's just being modest," Jessie said, jumping in. Jessie turned and pulled Meilin aside again. "C'mon!" she insisted with a hushed voice. "It's either this or cheerleading."

Meilin grit her teeth. "You're trying to kill me, right?" she whispered to her friend.

Jessie simply smiled.

Coach Daniels motioned for the other girls practicing their floor routines to clear the floor exercise area—all except Barbara, a junior and one of the team's seasoned gymnasts.

"Barb, show us a full-in—full-out," Coach Daniels said.

The athletic blond junior nodded and went into a short run that culminated into a dive into a forward handspring, two full twisting aerial somersaults and a reverse pike. She landed smartly on her feet, finishing her run with the typical gymnastics flair.

Coach Daniels nodded her approval before turning to Meilin. "Something there you can do?"

"Well, um," Meilin wavered.

"Piece of cake," Jessie said matter-of-factly.

"Great!" Coach Daniels motioned for Meilin to take the mat. "But since you're not warmed up, let's begin with a running walkover into a forward somie." She then called to Barbara, "Barb, spot Meilin for the somie."

Barbara nodded and moved to the center of the mat.

Coach Daniels then returned her attention to Meilin. "Whenever you're ready."

Meilin nodded. She then took a deep breath and ran. Meilin executed the walkover effortlessly and was only going to do the one forward somersault, but when her feet lifted off the ground and she spun through the air, something inside happened. It was a feeling of—pure joy. She soared through the air, touched down and immediately snapped into two reverse somies, and ended with a full pike, planting her feet just as Barbara had done to finish.

At least, that's what Meilin saw herself doing in her mind. With her demon monkey skills, she could easily do those moves and a whole lot more—moves that no gymnast could ever imagine. But she couldn't. Not here.

Instead, Meilin launched herself in the air for a forward somersault, finishing the tumble with the mat meeting her rear end with a tremendous WHOMP!

Everyone watching in the gym cringed.

"Ow!" was all Meilin could say.

Coach Daniels looked down at Jessie.

"Maybe it wasn't a somie she did last summer after all," Jessie shrugged.

"Maybe it wasn't," Coach Daniels returned with a wry smile. "And maybe you shouldn't try to front your friend. I have a feeling she can make it on her own."

"Sorry about the crummy spot," Barbara said, helping Meilin to her feet. "I thought you could jump higher."

"So did I," Meilin said as she rubbed her behind. She wasn't hurt, but had to act as if she was. "Good thing the ground broke my fall," she quipped for Barbara's benefit.

"All right," Coach Daniels said as Meilin rejoined them. "Any more cool moves you want your friend to demonstrate?" she directed at Jessie.

"No ma'am," Jessie said, catching Coach Daniels' drift. "Sorry, ma'am…"

"Good," Coach Daniels continued. Then, addressing her words to all the new girls, "We're all about safety here. That means learning the moves and routines safely and responsibly. There are no stars on this team—and *no* egos. We all work together and *with* each other. Yes, we will compete against other schools, but I tell you now, it's not about winning. I want you to think of gymnastics as a personal journey of mind and body. There's no rush. It takes a long time to develop your body's strength and control, but if you work hard, you'll be surprised at what you can achieve. Plus, it's a whole lot'a fun. So, if that's what you're here for," Coach Daniels glanced directly at Meilin and Jessie, "welcome to the team."

All the new girls nodded, including Jessie and Meilin. Perhaps this *was* something Meilin could lose herself in and enjoy. Meilin also saw Ms. Daniels in a new light. She sounded very much like her Uncle Zhu, or even crusty old Master Zhang—but without the grouchiness. Was there Tao in gymnastics? Mind. Body. Strength. Inner control. Was it about balance? Harmony? Indeed, it was!

A shrill whistle split the air.

It came from Coach Dan Taylor, the boys' gymnastics coach, as the boys team came trotting out from the locker room, ready to occupy their half of the gym. And with them was a familiar face—Connor Hunt.

"This sport just got better," Jessie said, nudging Meilin with an elbow.

Taylor walked over to Coach Daniels while the boys began their warm-ups. He was a burly man, bald, a retired police sergeant turned gym coach. He drove his boys hard and expected results—a far different approach to coaching than Daniels'.

"How's the team shaping up?" he said with a gruff voice.

"I think we have a good group of girls," Coach Daniels replied.

"Same. Especially with my new addition," he said pointing in Connor's direction. "We could go as far as State with him.

Coach Daniels nodded slightly as she and the rest of the girls watched Connor position himself under the rings. A teammate hoisted him up and he gripped the rings and started his routine. He easily muscled up to a straddled "L" position and then smoothly pressed that up to a handstand. The rings hardly wavered, showing he had good control and balance. From there he did two back giants into handstands, which he then lowered into an iron cross.

"Whoa," Jessie said under her breath. "He's totally ripped!"

"I'll say," Meilin uttered softly, equally impressed.

"See what I mean?" Coach Taylor smiled to Daniels. "State, all the way!" he said as he walked back to his boys.

Still holding the iron cross, Connor looked across the gym to where Meilin and Jessie were standing. Recognizing Meilin, he quickly went into a giant swing to a flying dismount. He then came trotting quickly toward them.

"Hey, Meilin!" he called.

"Hey," Meilin answered. The two stared at each other for a moment in awkward silence. Jessie nudged Meilin slightly. "Oh, this is my best friend, Jessie."

Connor nodded and smiled. "Hi, Jess."

"Hi," Jessie returned with a wide smile.

"Um, about yesterday," Meilin and Connor said in unison.

"I just wanted to say..." they both said awkwardly together again. The two then laughed.

"Sorry, you first," Connor said.

Meilin shrugged. "Okay, I just wanted to say I'm sorry about what happened and see if you were all right. I tried to catch you this morning, but you were with Tiffany so I didn't get the chance..."

"Yeah, she's a pushy girl. Really starting to bug me. But as far as yesterday goes, totally not your fault," Connor replied.

"But your arms," Meilin countered.

"Just a couple'a scratches, see?" Connor replied holding his forearms up to his chest so both girls could have a look. Indeed, the girls could see that the many places where the shards of flying glass from the exploding beaker had pierced his skin were remarkably healed over.

"See? It looked worse than it actually was," he continued.

"I just don't know how it happened," Meilin said.

"Me either," Connor replied, "But..."

A shrill blast from Coach Taylor's whistle interrupted.

"Hunt! Let's go!" he shouted from across the gym.

Connor rolled his eyes. "Well, gotta go," he said. As he turned to leave, "Hey, you wanna get a slice or something after school with me sometime?"

That caught Meilin by surprise!

"Well, um," she hesitated.

"Now, Hunt!" Coach Taylor shouted again.

"Yes!" Jessie, butted in, answering for her friend. "She'd love to."

"Cool, how about tonight?" Connor grinned. Vinny's Sub Shop? Six o'clock?"

"She'll be there!" Jessie answered for Meilin again.

Connor looked at both Meilin and Jessie. He snorted a smile then turned and trotted back to his teammates.

"Rule number one," Meilin could hear Coach Taylor grumble. "Girls team—off limits!"

Jessie and Meilin stared at each other for a long moment, then bobbed up and down.

"Eee! You got a date!" Jessie squealed with hushed delight.

"Eee! I got a date!" Meilin replied with equal glee. Then she paused as it sunk in. "OMG, I got a date!" Her first date. What should she do? What should she wear? What would her mother say? Worse, what would Uncle Zhu say?

Chapter 10

"**A**bsolutely not!" Zhu Bajie bellowed, retracting his head from the kitchen refrigerator. He was in the middle of making dinner for them both when Meilin told him about her *date* with Connor.

"No way! Uh-uh! Nadda! Nyet! Nein! Nope! And No!" he continued, making certain that there was no question as to his position on the matter.

"But Uncle Z!" Meilin complained.

"You're too young!"

"I'm fourteen!"

"Like I said—too young!"

"Uncle Z!"

"When you're sixty, I'll think about it!"

"It's just a slice of pizza," Meilin argued. "Besides, he's nice!"

"How do you know? You just met him!"

"I just know!" Meilin countered.

"Sorry!"

"It's not fair!" Meilin cried.

"Yup!" Zhu Bajie stated flatly. "But that's the way it is. You have schoolwork to do, midterms are coming up—and there's your training!"

"Other kids my age have boyfriends!"

"You're not *other* kids!" Zhu Bajie countered. "You're Princess Meilin of Shuilian-dong—daughter of the Monkey King! You're not the same as other people!"

Tears suddenly welled in Meilin's eyes. "Because I'm half-monkey?"

"Of course not," Zhu Bajie replied. But it was too late. The words were said and he couldn't take them back.

"Yes it is! It's because I'm different! I'm a freak!"

With tears streaming down her face, Meilin turned and ran up the stairs to her bedroom and slammed the door.

"Meilin!" Zhu Bajie called. But there was no reply. "Stupid, Pigsy! Stupid! Stupid!" he growled, admonishing himself. He touched the one nerve he knew Meilin couldn't yet handle—her identity.

Zhu Bajie ascended the stairs and knocked softly on her door.

"Meilin..." he called.

"Go away!" her voice trembled through the door.

"C'mon, Meilin. You know I didn't mean it like that," Zhu Bajie replied.

"Go—away!" Meilin said more forcibly.

Zhu Bajie exhaled. There was nothing he could do or say that would make things better—at least not at the moment. "I'll let you know when dinner's ready," he said.

No reply.

Zhu Bajie shook his weary head, slowly turned, and went back downstairs. He wished Lijuan were home. This was definitely an issue that required the loving care of a mother—not a bumbling demon pig.

Meilin paced back and forth in her room. She was furious with her uncle. She was more furious with herself. Why couldn't she be like other girls and live a normal life? She didn't ask to be the Monkey King's daughter. If there was a way she could give it all up, she gladly would. But there wasn't. Life didn't work that way.

Meilin stared at herself in the mirror over her dresser next to her bed. Through her watery eyes, two reflections stared back at her—one human, and one demon monkey. She wiped her eyes with her shirtsleeve and the reflections resolved into her normal appearance.

She then looked at the digital clock on her dresser. It read, 5:30.

"If life deals you lemons, make lemonade," she said to herself with sudden determination.

Meilin went to her window, threw it open and looked down at the grass below. It was a good twenty-five foot drop, one she could easily do without injury. But her window was almost directly above the kitchen. If she jumped down, her uncle might spot her.

Instead, Meilin decided to take a different route. She wanted to get to Jessie's house, and the most direct way was along the line of trees that loosely spanned and connected their respective backyards.

Meilin was the Monkey King's daughter, so why not make good use of it?

Why not, indeed!

Meilin morphed herself into a squirrel, jumped out of her window, and scampered along the branches. Within minutes, she was perched on the windowsill outside Jessie's bedroom.

Jessie was busy with her homework and listening to music on her *iPod* when she heard a faint tapping sound on the glass. She turned and looked. Her eyes widened with disgust.

"Shoo!" she cried, grabbing her notebook and waving it menacingly at the squirrel. "Get outta here! Dang roof rat!"

But the squirrel didn't budge. Instead, it stood on its hind legs and made an *open the window* gesture with its two tiny paws.

"Meilin?" Jessie said with a look of dumfounded realization.

The squirrel nodded its head and waved her over.

"OMG!" Jessie said as she opened her window. Meilin jumped inside and immediately morphed back into herself.

"We have a front door, ya know," Jessie remarked.

"I didn't want anyone to see me."

"Why, what's up?"

Meilin told her about the argument she had with her uncle.

"So what do you wanna do?" Jessie asked.

"I wanna keep the date."

"But your uncle said..." Jessie countered.

"I don't care!" Meilin interrupted. "I need a break from my life. I want to go see Connor, and I want you to come with me!"

"Me?" Jessie said.

"Yes!" Meilin said. "C'mon, you're my BFF and I need you. I mean, what if I don't know what to say..."

"Yeah, but..."

"Please?" Meilin implored her friend.

"Okay," Jessie said. "But don't yell at me when your uncle finds out."

"He won't find out," Meilin replied. "We'll walk to Vinny's, have a slice and be back home in an hour—ninety minutes, tops!"

"We better be," Jessie said. "Otherwise, I'll be in hot water myself."

"I promise," Meilin said.

Jessie plucked her *iPod nano* from her desk, stuffed it into her back pocket and went for her bedroom door. Meilin followed.

"Whoa!" Jessie said. "You can't go downstairs. You're not here, remember?"

"Oh yeah," Meilin returned. "I'll meet you by the big tree in the front yard."

Meilin then morphed herself back into a squirrel and hopped up on the windowsill.

"Watch out for Cookie!" Jessie called before Meilin disappeared. "She hates squirrels."

Chapter 11

"Hey," Connor said, flashing a smile as Meilin and Jessie approached. He was standing outside the door to Vinny's Sub Shop next to several parked cars. It was only 6pm, but already the late November sky was darkening. "I was beginning to think you weren't coming," he said.

"Sorry I'm late," Meilin replied. "Hope you don't mind that Jessie came along," she added.

Connor shrugged, "The more the merrier."

"Waiting long?" Meilin asked.

"Not long. Had my tunes to keep me company," Connor returned as he took the mini earplugs that dangled loosely around his neck and tucked them into the front pocket of the dark red windbreaker he was wearing.

"Cool," Jessie said. "What ya listenin' to?

"A little *Alicia Keys*, some *Foo Fighters*, *Chevelle*, a bit of hip-hop. I kind'a like to mix it up."

"Me too!" Jessie smiled.

"How about you?" Connor asked, looking at Meilin.

"The same as Jess," Meilin said. "Well, until I lost my *iPod*," she added, giving Jessie an apologetic frown.

"Bummer," Connor noted.

The three stood in awkward silence for the next few seconds, not knowing what to say.

"Well, um..." Connor finally said.

"Pizza," Jessie quickly chirped for Meilin's benefit.

"Right, pizza," Connor replied. He then gestured toward the sub shop's door, opening it for both girls to enter.

The tiny sub shop wasn't crowded so they grabbed an empty table near the large plate glass windows that lined the front of the shop.

While Connor went to order some slices, Jessie turned to Meilin.

"C'mon! Say something interesting to him," she half-whispered.

"Like what?" Meilin returned.

"Something—anything or he's gonna think you're a complete doof."

"I am a doof," Meilin said. "And I shouldn't be sitting here. This whole thing's a mistake."

"Oh, great!" Jessie remarked. "You're on a date with the hottest guy in school and you wanna go home?"

"You should be the one sitting here, not me," Meilin said.

"That's the monkey in you talking. Besides, it's obvious he likes you. Look, we're here now, and I'm hungry!" Jessie said. "Rule number 16 of the Jessie Macintyre Dating Guide—eat first, eat big, *then* bail."

Meilin snorted a short laugh. "Jess, you've never been on a date, either."

"And your point is?" Jessie countered with a smile. Jessie then nudged Meilin under the table with her foot, signaling Connor's impending return.

"Hope you like mushroom," he said, arriving with a plastic tray laden with several slices of pizza and three medium-sized root beers.

Meilin and Jessie nodded as he sat.

"Good, 'cause that's all they had ready," he grinned as he passed each girl their slices on paper plates.

Meilin picked up her slice and was about to bite into it went Jessie nudged her under the table with her foot again. Meilin shot her a *"what?"* look.

"Meilin and I we're talking about...gymnastics," Jessie said, giving Meilin the opportunity to continue the conversation.

"Yes, well, um," Meilin began, "It was surprising to see you there. More surprising to see how really good you are."

"Nah, not really," Connor said modestly. "I took it up a few years ago to keep my mind focused on something physical. With all the moving around my Dad does, I had to do something to keep from going crazy. Constantly changing schools isn't any fun. So, when I got here and learned they had a team, I signed up. And then I saw you," he said, looking at Meilin, "and it was like, wow— somebody I know does it too."

"Oh," Meilin said shyly. "Well, it was really Jessie's idea." She then looked down at the table, staring at her uneaten slice, as she tried to think of something else to say. She could comment about the weather—but that'd be dumb. Or even talk about music again, but they already did that. *Talk about being off center with her Tao—why was this so hard?* Connor was just a boy, the same as any other boy she knew. Sure he was hot and all, but still, just a boy. What would Uncle Z say?

"The snow goose need not bathe to make itself white. Neither need you do anything but be yourself." That's what he'd say. Another one of Lao Tzu's fortune cookie wisdoms, and he'd be right, as usual. But being yourself was hard, especially when one part of you was demon monkey. Who was the real Meilin? That was the million-dollar question and the one Meilin couldn't yet answer.

"I'm sorry," Meilin said as she suddenly stood. "We should go. Thanks for the pizza..."

"Oh?" Connor said with surprise. "Did I say something wrong?"

Jessie gave Meilin a quizzical look, as well.

"No," Meilin replied. "I just remembered that I have a lot of homework to do..." In reality, she was thinking of Uncle Z and the way she left things with him.

"It's not because I was hanging with Tiffany at school, is it? I mean, I really don't like her and I know she doesn't like you—she's just like— everywhere I turn, she's always there." Connor said, searching for a better reason as to why Meilin didn't want to stay.

"No, it's not that," Meilin insisted. "I really do have homework..."

"At least let me walk you home," Connor countered.

"No, that's okay, Meilin said.

"Halfway then," Connor insisted. "I live a couple of blocks from here so I'm going that way."

"That'd be great," Jessie said, butting in. She shot Meilin a *what's wrong with you* look.

"Okay," Meilin relented, just to make her friend happy.

Conner nodded and smiled again. He had a warm smile, Meilin had to admit. And maybe she did like him more than a little bit, but everything was just too confusing for her right now. She needed time to sort things out in her mind—time to find her center.

It was now dark as the three walked along the sidewalk past the many shops and stores that had already closed for the night.

"It's chilly," Jessie remarked, shivering slightly. "Should'a brought my jacket."

"Here, take mine," Connor said, slipping his windbreaker off and handing it to Jessie.

"Meilin?" Jessie asked, wondering if her friend was cold.

Meilin shook her head. "I'm fine," she said. She was. The cool night air didn't bother her.

"Thanks," Jessie said as she draped the windbreaker around her shoulders.

"My parents and I live on East River Street," Connor said as they passed a narrow alley that was littered with old paint cans and trash that cut between a paint shop and a dry cleaners. "Do you have time to say hello? They'd be happy to see I've made a few new friends. My Dad can even drive you home."

"Maybe some other time," Meilin said.

"A ride home sounds good to me," Jessie countered.

Meilin grimaced slightly, but could see that Jessie was indeed cold. "Okay, but we can't stay long."

"Great," Connor said. "We can cut through here," he said turning into the alley.

As they walked, Jessie unconsciously reached into the front pocket of Connor's jacket and fished out his *iPod.* "Mind if I look at your song list? Maybe we can share some..." Jessie stopped mid-sentence. "OMG, Meilin!"

Meilin turned and saw that Jessie was holding a magenta *iPod nano* in her hands. It didn't take more than a heartbeat for her to realize that it was hers.

In a flash, Connor circled behind Jessie. His left arm wrapped around her neck, lifting her slightly off the ground, choking her. With his free hand, he plucked the *iPod* from her grasp. "You weren't supposed to see that!" he growled.

Immediately Meilin's instincts took over and she morphed into her demon monkey state.

"Uh-uh, Princess!" Connor warned. "I'll snap her neck before you can even move!" he added, tightening his iron grip around Jessie's neck. Her eyes bulged and her face turned beet-red as she struggled for air.

"Who are you!" Meilin demanded, backing off.

"My name's not important," Connor hissed. "What *is* important is that I've got an old score to settle!"

"What score? I don't even know you!"

"Oh, but your father does! He cost me 600 years of my life. Now it's payback time!"

"But how..." Meilin started.

"...Did I find you?" Connor finished for her. "Easy! All it took was a little gold and a flea-bitten Huli-jing to get me this," he said with a contemptuous laugh as he displayed Meilin's magenta *iPod nano* in his right hand. "A homing beacon to the here and now!"

Connor's right hand then erupted into a fiery fist of blue flame! Meilin's iPod nano instantly disintegrated in his hand. "Say good-bye to your monkey friend!" Connor whispered into Jessie's ear as he threw a massive ball of deadly blue flame straight at Meilin's face.

Chapter 12

With a tremendous "Hee-ya!" Zhu Bajie's nine-toothed rake of pure ice-metal smacked the flaming ball of death Connor threw at Meilin high into the night sky, mere moments before it struck her square in her face. The huge demon pig then twirled his rake in an attempt to sweep Connor's legs out from under him before he could launch another attack.

With the sudden appearance of her uncle, Meilin snapped into action as well. Her longest jade hair stick flew into her hand from her ponytail knot and instantly morphed to bo staff size. She quickly leapt forward to attack.

But Connor anticipated both their moves. He flew backwards, avoiding Zhu Bajie's rake sweep and Meilin's bo attack to his ribs. His eyes glowed with blue rage as he still held Jessie like a rag doll, helpless in his grasp.

"I'm not *that* easy!" he sneered. This time, two bolts of blue fire spit from his eyes, again straight at Meilin.

Meilin parried each fireball with her bo, redirecting each into the brick building beside Connor. The bricks exploded and the wall went up in blue flame. The impact of the blasts rocked the building so hard that it set off the internal burglar and fire alarms.

"Not bad," Connor laughed. "But you'll have to do better than that!"

Again he unleashed a blue fireball from his free hand. Instead of directing it at Meilin, he aimed it at the ground surrounding both Meilin and Zhu Bajie. The asphalt pavement in the alley exploded with a blaze of blue fire. The fire licked at Meilin's legs. Zhu Bajie threw himself on the ground in front of his niece saving her from being burned. The fire enveloped Zhu Bajie and he rolled around wildly in an effort to put the flames out.

"Uncle Z!" Meilin screamed helplessly as the fire consumed him.

Then abruptly, the fire vanished, leaving Zhu Bajie's clothes tattered and blackened. Miraculously, his body was only slightly singed.

Connor laughed maniacally. "Is that roast pig I smell?"

"What do you want!" Meilin demanded.

"Isn't it obvious?" Connor growled. "I want *you*—dead!"

"Then fight me!" Meilin snapped angrily. "Quit hiding behind Jessie and fight me. Or are you a coward!"

Connor laughed. "Ooo, I'm a coward," he snorted mockingly. He laughed again. "Okay," he said releasing Jessie and shoving her forward. "You can have your stupid little friend back."

Jessie ran toward Meilin and Zhu Bajie, terrified for her life. Zhu Bajie grabbed her outstretched hand and pulled her behind him so he could shield her with his body.

"And we'll fight. But not here!" Connor said. "Beating you here is too easy. It wouldn't mean anything. I want the world to see—*our world* to see!"

"And if I don't come?"

"Oh, you'll come," Connor said as a magical vortex to the past materialized behind him. Before he stepped through, he smiled his warm Connor-smile, "I hear Shuilian-dong is nice this time of year..."

Meilin's jaw tightened with both anger and fear. Her mother was in Shuilian-dong. Was he going to go after her? And what about the rest of monkey-kind who lived there? Could they stave off his fiery attack?

Connor winked at Meilin as he stepped backward through the vortex and vanished.

"Ahhh!" Meilin screamed with utter frustration. She whirled and looked at her uncle. Smoke was still rising off of his clothes and skin. If Zhu Bajie weren't immortal, he'd be dead.

The look in Meilin's eyes demanded an explanation, but there was no time for that now. Fast-approaching sirens could be heard. And there was Jessie. They had to get her out of here, make sure she wasn't injured and get her home.

Zhu Bajie conjured a cloud large enough for three and in an instant they shot straight up into the night sky as two police cars, their lights flashing blue and red, rolled into the alley.

Chapter 13

"It's called Samadhi Fire," Zhu Bajie said, sitting on a chair at the kitchen table of their home.

"Samadhi?" Meilin remarked, as she set a large bowl of ice cubes and water in front of her uncle. Inside the bowl was a white washcloth. She wrung it out and gently applied it to the burned skin around his face.

"Divine fire," Zhu Bajie continued, grimacing with some degree of pain. "It's the holiest of fires, impossible to extinguish even with water. This guy's twisted it into something evil."

"How?" Meilin wanted to know. "Who *is* he? And what's his problem?"

"Yeah," Jessie chimed in. She was shaken from the ordeal, but remarkably uninjured. Meilin and Zhu Bajie wanted her to go home but she refused to leave until she was certain Zhu was okay.

"His name is Hong Hai-Er—the Red Boy."

"Hong Hai-Er?" Meilin repeated. "The name sounds familiar.

"It should," Zhu Bajie replied. "He's the son of the Demon Bull King!"

"OMG!" Meilin said, stunned with the revelation. "No wonder he hates my father."

"Ya think?" Zhu Bajie snorted.

"Hey," Jessie interrupted. "Newbie here... Wanna bring me up to speed with the family history? After all, he wanted to roast me, too!"

Zhu Bajie shook his weary head, but complied. Jessie deserved to know who almost killed her and Zhu was never one to pass up telling a story.

"It was during our Journey to the West," he began. "We needed to cross the Fiery Mountains of Bull King's domain. But Bull King had placed the mountains under his son's control. Your father politely asked if Hong Hai-Er would extinguish the flames so we might continue our pilgrimage for the Sacred Scrolls, but he refused. One thing led to another and a fight ensued. Were it not for Sun Wukong's ability to withstand Samadhi fire, he would have been killed. Still, he was severely injured."

Zhu Bajie turned his head painfully toward Meilin. "This was the only time I've ever seen your father almost defeated. Where it not for Guanyin's intervention, I doubt we would have prevailed."

"The Goddess of Mercy," Jessie interjected.

Zhu Bajie nodded. "She entrapped Hong Hai-Er with five golden bands, binding his hands, wrists, head and legs. She then cast a spell that fixed his arms and hands to his chest, immobilizing him so he could do no more than bow his head and kowtow. It was relatively simple to extinguish the flames after your father secured the magic Banana Leaf Fan from Hong Hai-Er's mother, Tie Shan Gongzhu, Princess Iron Fan—but how he managed to do that is a story for another day."

"So what's next?" Jessie asked.

Zhu Bajie looked at Jessie and smiled. "What's next is you go home, get some rest and try to forget what happened tonight."

"But," Jessie started to say, then stopped. She knew there was nothing she could do to help. All of this was beyond her. She looked at Meilin. "You be careful," she said standing. She hugged Meilin close. "Come back, ya hear?"

Meilin nodded and returned her friend's embrace.

Chapter 14

The doors of the magical wooden Chinese Gate standing within Water Curtain Cave flew open. Meilin, in her full demon monkey form, and Zhu Bajie stepped through the vortex that connected the future to the past, neither sure what to expect. What they saw horrified them.

Fires burned everywhere. And everywhere Meilin turned, she saw demon monkey soldiers lying on the ground, many severely burned. The monkey-children, too, did not escape the attack.

"*Meilin,*" they cried when they saw her, calling for her comfort and her help.

Meilin burst into tears. She knelt and carefully picked up one of the children and cradled her close. It was one of the little girls who had pressed a flower into her hand only a few days ago.

"Meilin," she barely managed to whisper. "I can't...play with you...today..."

Meilin stared up at Zhu Bajie with despair. "This is all my fault," she was scarcely able to croak through her tears.

"You didn't do this," Zhu Bajie returned.

"Yes, I did. I was careless..."

"Shh!" Zhu Bajie hushed softly. "Meilin, I need you to focus. Right now, we have to do everything we can to help!"

"What can we do?" Meilin started. Then she paused and shouted, "Mom!"

In a distant corner of the cave, Lijuan stood up from the wounded demon monkey she was attending.

"Meilin! Zhu!" she cried as she ran over. "Thank heaven you're both here! Zhu, I need you to go into the mountains and get me more herbs. Take two of the shamans with you. They'll know what I need!"

"I'm on it!" Zhu Bajie replied, racing off as fast as his massive body could move.

"Meilin, I need you to help me wrap the burn victims with the strips of cloth I've already soaked with medicine."

"What about the children?" Meilin cried. "We have to save them!"

"Children first, of course!" Lijuan replied. She was cool, calm and collected—in every way a Queen. There was work to do and she was right in the thick of it, leading the way, using every ounce of her energy and healing skill to help her people. Meilin was never more proud of her mother in her life than at that moment. Could she ever be like her?

"Quickly!" Lijuan urged. "Every second matters! Have the children brought to you and wrap them."

Meilin did as her mother ordered. She carefully wrapped every child in medicine-soaked bandages as fast as they were carried to her. When she ran low on bandages, she ripped strips of cloth from her own clothing and soaked them until more bandages could be found. She worked furiously for hours until, finally, each and every child was bandaged and secure. Those that needed comforting, she held close to her chest and sang into their ears the lullaby her mother used to sing to her when she was very young until the medicine her mother prepared to ease their pain allowed them to sleep.

"You-you-zha. You-you-zha," Meilin sang softly in Mandarin, tears streaming down her face. "Ma ma de bao bao shui jiao ba ... Bai hua shu pi ya, zuo yao lan ba bu zha ... *Hush, little baby, go to sleep... In your cradle of bark from the white birch tree... Even if a wolf, tiger, or demon comes, have no fear... High in the white mountain, where the water runs deep, you are safe... When you grow up, you'll become a hero."*

With every child Meilin held and with every lullaby she sang, her heart broke until it could break no more. It was only then, through the grief and utter despair that surrounded her, that she finally realized who she was.

"I *am* monkey!" Meilin said out loud to herself.

"Yes, you are," Zhu Bajie said from behind. "And a whole lot more! You are Meilin, the Monkey King's daughter. And your people need you, just as much as they need your mother."

Zhu Bajie gently turned Meilin around to face him.

"Are you finally ready to find your center and fully embrace your Tao?"

"Yes, Uncle, I am," Meilin said solemnly.

"Good," Zhu Bajie replied. "Then it's time to prepare."

Chapter 15

"I absolutely forbid it!" Lijuan stated firmly. Her gaze shifted from Zhu Bajie to Meilin then back to Zhu Bajie. "And *you*—how could you even suggest such a thing!"

"There *is* no other way," Zhu Bajie replied. "If Meilin doesn't face Hong Hai-Er, he'll surely return—if not to Shuilian-dong, then to some other unsuspecting village or town, and wreak the same havoc upon them."

"You seriously think I'd allow my daughter to risk her life!" Lijuan glared.

"It's *my* life," Meilin rebutted.

"Meilin!" Lijuan countered. "You don't even know what you're saying!"

"Yes, I do!" Meilin said forcibly. "I'm doing the same thing you're doing. Saving our people!" Then she added with conviction, "*My* people. *My* family."

"You're father would never allow..." Lijuan began, but Meilin cut her off.

"Dad's not here!" Meilin argued. "If he were, this wouldn't have happened. But he's not. So, it's up to me!"

"But you're just a child."

"No, Mom—I'm not! I'm fourteen! I know who I am! I accept it!" Meilin said. Then she added in a softer voice, "Besides, I'm the only one. You can't fight. I can!"

"Zhu!" Lijuan implored, hoping to find some voice of reason and support from him. But the huge demon pig could only shrug. It was clear that he agreed with Meilin. This was the only option. If Meilin didn't face Hong Hai-Er, he would burn and destroy other villages until she did.

"I *am* my father's daughter. I have his powers! You've said so, yourself!" Meilin stated in an effort to reinforce her position. This was true, but to what extent was still unknown. Was she born with *all* of Sun Wukong's powers, or just a few? That was a question that might never be answered. Meilin would never know what powers she inherited from her father until they manifested in her—and this only seemed to happen if and when some internal or external catalyst, such as extreme danger, triggered them.

Sun Wukong could perform all 72 Transformations at will, knew hundreds of charms and magic spells, was both skilled in every form of martial art and undefeatable in battle. He was also invulnerable and, most importantly, he was immortal.

Meilin was neither invulnerable nor immortal. She didn't know any spells or charms and as yet had rarely tried to transform herself into something else, such as a squirrel. As for her fighting ability, this seemed to come intuitively to her, but then again, only when needed. So, could she prevail against Hong Hai-Er? Would some new aspect of her powers kick in when needed? Or was what had already manifested in her the extent of all there would ever be? If this were the case, then she would lose. Still, it was a chance she had to take. She needed to believe she could defeat Hong Hai-Er, even if how to do so was not, at the moment, clear to her.

Lijuan still wasn't onboard. "I've already sent word to the Jade Emperor to recall your father."

"You know he won't do that!" Zhu Bajie replied. "Sun Wukong is on a secret Imperial mission. Bull King still conspires against the kingdom. To even try to locate Wukong now could cause even more damage than what occurred here."

Lijuan grit her teeth.

"There *is* no other option," Zhu Bajie restated. "She *must* face him."

"There's *always* another option to violence," Lijuan said. *"Always!"*

"Your Highness!" a demon monkey shaman interrupted. "There are complications with some of the children. We need you."

Meilin's heart jumped. Some of the children were in trouble. Which ones? Were her mother's treatments not working? Or were some of the injured beyond her ability to be helped at all!

"This discussion isn't over," Lijuan declared, before hurrying off with the shaman to the chamber in the cave where the children were hospitalized.

Meilin started after her mother, but Zhu Bajie stayed her. "Your mother will handle this," he said.

"But..." Meilin protested, wanting to be of some help to her mother.

"Trust me," Zhu Bajie said. "Your mother is a more powerful healer than you know. The children are in good hands with her. You have another responsibility to take care of.

Meilin slowly nodded. Zhu Bajie was right.

"When do we leave?" Meilin asked.

"We don't. You do," Zhu Bajie responded.

"W-what!" Meilin stuttered with disbelief. "You're not coming with me?"

"No," Zhu Bajie stated. "I have something else to do."

"Then who?" Meilin asked, worried that without the support of her uncle, she wouldn't know what to do.

"Me!" a voice behind her said.

Meilin turned in place to face the familiar voice. It was Xiao-Hong—the Huli-jing who betrayed her at the start.

"I—will come with you!"

Chapter 16

"You!" Meilin growled. She glared at the Huli-jing who stood before her with absolute contempt. Her longest jade hair stick flew into her hands as it morphed to bo staff size. "This is all *your* fault! Tell me why I shouldn't send you straight to hell where you belong!"

"If that's your wish," Xiao-Hong replied calmly, "I won't contest it." The Huli-jing stood before Meilin, still wrapped head-to-toe in the bandages that Lijuan applied to her when she first arrived. Only her piercing black eyes could be seen through the wrappings that completely covered her face.

Meilin's muscles tensed with raw anger as she raised her bo staff to strike Xiao-Hong down—but found she couldn't. She couldn't kill the Huli-jing, even though she was partially responsible for what had happened. That wasn't her Tao.

Meilin stared into Xiao-Hong's eyes. They showed no remorse for what she did or for what had subsequently transpired. "You really don't have a soul, do you," Meilin said with pity as she lowered her jade bo staff.

"No," Xiao-Hong replied. "That's our nature. And that's why you must let me help you."

"Help me?" Meilin said with incredulity. "First you befriend me—then you betray me—and now you want to help me? Why should I believe you!"

"Because I can teach you how to survive the Samadhi fire!"

That statement caught Meilin by surprise. She turned her head toward her uncle. Zhu Bajie nodded. Meilin returned her gaze to the Huli-jing.

"The only reason I didn't die from Hong Hai-Er's attack was because at the last moment, I was able to morph into my spirit-fox form," Xiao-Hong said. "Even then, it was almost too late."

"How can simply turning into a fox do that?" Meilin smirked.

"Spirit-fox," Zhu Bajie interjected. "She's talking about entering the Shadow Realm."

"Shadow Realm?" Meilin repeated, still not understanding the significance of her uncle's words.

"The realm of wraiths and ghosts," Xiao-Hong stated flatly.

"Think of it as another dimension, slightly out of sync with ours," Zhu Bajie explained, putting it in modern terms Meilin could better understand. "But in order to cross over to that realm, you'll need to learn Shadow Magic."

Meilin's eyes widened. "But that's dark magic! Won't that make me..."

"Evil?" Xiao-Hong finished for her. "Don't confuse evil with darkness. They're not the same. You succumb to evil only if you surrender to it. My kind embraced darkness long ago, which is why we feed on the souls of men. That does not make us evil. We follow our nature, our Tao—just as you follow yours. This is not to say that the path you choose is without consequence. For you, the path to enlightenment is still open. For us, it's not."

Meilin stared at the Huli-jing for several moments. "I don't trust you. For all I know, you're just setting me up again."

"I'm not!" Xiao-Hong said. "Because your mother saved my life, I'm honor-bound to her until the day I die. That includes preserving all that she loves."

"Ha!" Meilin snorted. "This—from someone who's incapable of loving anything."

Xiao-Hong didn't answer. Instead, she began to remove the bandages from her body—first her arms, then her legs, torso and abdomen—and lastly, her face.

Meilin stared at the Huli-jing with both disbelief and amazement. She wasn't the striking fox-like beauty Meilin knew her to be. Her face and body, though not hideously disfigured, bore the harsh scars of the fire. What was most disturbing was her fur. It wasn't red-grey anymore. Her fur and her long hair had turned pure white.

"As you can see, I'm no longer the Huli-jing I once was."

"I'm sorry," Meilin said. And she was. But, Meilin's feelings didn't alter the fact that Xiao-Hong was still a Huli-jing inside. The Samadhi fire had not changed that.

"In order to enter the Shadow Realm, you must be able to fully embrace your Yin," Zhu Bajie began. "Embrace it, but not give in to it. If you do, you risk being lost in it forever."

"But Uncle Z," Meilin replied. "You taught me that Yin and Yang are inseparable, each complementing the other."

"True," Zhu Bajie continued. "Neither exists without the other. But pure Yin itself is not evil. Nor is pure Yang, its counterpart, good. They're both aspects of the Whole. To embrace either alone will take you off your center—your place of Balance. When that happens, you will not be following your Tao."

"Then how do I embrace only my Yin without losing myself in darkness?" Meilin asked.

"By understanding that Yin *is* Yang and Yang *is* Yin," Zhu Bajie returned. "You must empty your mind of all worldly distraction to fully embrace the essence of the Tao. Only when your empty mind becomes a mirror of the Tao, will you be able to transform and equalize your Yin and Yang, one into the other, so that your Balance is restored. If you can master that without conscious thought, the path to true Enlightenment is open to you."

Meilin shook her head with frustration. "Why do I feel as if I'm having a *Yoda* moment here?"

"*Yoda*? What's a *Yoda*?" Xiao-Hong asked.

"Funny little green guy with long ears. Says everything kind'a backwards," Meilin said. She gazed at the bewildered Huli-jing. "It's a future thing. Forget I even mentioned it."

Xiao-Hong snorted and stepped forward. She took Meilin's hands in hers. The Huli-jing's hands were ice cold and Meilin's first reaction was to snatch her own hands back, but the demon fox's words stayed her.

"Follow me," she said calmly. "Embrace the darkness of the Tao and follow me."

Meilin tried to do as Xiao-Hong requested, but her Yang was strong and she couldn't let go. She was afraid to step off the comfort of her own center.

"Don't fight it," Xiao-Hong whispered. "Flow with it—into it—like water. Shape it to your will."

Meilin redoubled her efforts—and then it happened. She could feel her inner Tao begin to change. She felt herself slipping away—slipping far off her center—to the point where she felt like she was falling.

Suddenly, the Shadow Realm became visible to her.

With Xiao-Hong at her side, she crossed over.

The Shadow Realm was cold—completely devoid of any warmth, and, Meilin could feel, it was a world without any compassion or kindness in it at all. It was a world of sorrow and despair.

Meilin also sensed that the Shadow Realm was not an empty world. It had substance and form, perhaps even an odd beauty of its own.

"No!" Meilin's rational mind cried. This was a horrible place. A place she wanted no part of. But now that she was here, how could she get back? How could she return to her own world? She was immersed in Yin and it was beginning to feel good

to her. The darkness was feeling *good*—and that scared her.

"Meilin," she heard her uncle call. His disembodied words sounded distorted. She turned to look at him. He looked strange, almost ethereal to her.

In his hands, Zhu Bajie held his nine-toothed rake, poised to strike.

Strike, he did.

Zhu Bajie's rake came down on her neck. But instead of breaking her neck and crushing her to the ground, the rake of pure ice metal passed through her body as if she was made of smoke and mist. And she was. Meilin was a wraith.

Zhu Bajie then shouldered his rake and smiled.

"Come back!" he urged, his hands motioning to Meilin to return to her natural world.

"I-I can't!" she stammered.

"You can!" Zhu Bajie shouted. "Find your center!"

"Yin is Yang. Yang is Yin," Xiao-Hong whispered softly. "One flows into the other."

"Yin is Yang. Yang is Yin. One flows into the other," Meilin repeated to herself as she closed her eyes and focused all her will on that one thought. "Yin is Yang. Yang is Yin... One flows into the other... Yin is Yang. Yang is Yin... One flows into the other..."

Meilin felt herself slipping once again.

She collapsed—falling into her uncle's arms.

"Welcome back," he whispered, holding her close so that his massive body could warm hers. "Welcome back..."

Chapter 17

"I *never* want to do that again!" Meilin declared, still shivering from her ordeal. She looked up at her uncle as the three of them made their way across the monkey bridge that connected Water Curtain Cave to the world outside.

"You may have no choice," Zhu Bajie said. "Samadhi fire is confined to this world. Entering the Shadow Realm may be your only defense."

"Great..." Meilin grumbled.

The trio soon stood at the edge of the pool near the base of the spectacular waterfall that concealed the entrance to Shuilian-dong. The memory of Jessie swimming and demon monkey-children frolicking on the banks and playing in the shallows of the waters flooded her mind. Her eyes unexpectedly filled with tears again.

"Don't worry," Zhu Bajie said, as if he could read her mind. "The children will be all right. Your mother's with them."

Meilin nodded as she sniffled and wiped her eyes with her hand. She wasn't ashamed of her feelings—or her tears. Not anymore.

She turned to her uncle. "You told me Hong Hai-Er was imprisoned. Why is he free?"

"Time off for good behavior, I guess," Zhu Bajie replied. "After all, your grandmother *is* the Goddess of Mercy. After 600 years, perhaps she decided that he had suffered enough and was sufficiently reformed. Even your father was once imprisoned under a mountain for 500 years for peeing on Buddha's hand. Guanyin freed him after he agreed to join the monk, Xuanzang, and his pilgrimage to the West for the Sacred Scrolls."

"Well, she should'a saw this one coming," Meilin stated. "Which reminds me, why couldn't I? In school, in the gym—at the sub shop," she added sheepishly.

"Ah yes, the sub shop," Zhu Bajie said with a disapproving tone.

"You knew?"

"A little squirrel told me," he replied. "And lucky for you she did. Seems you were in her tree…"

"All right, I'm sorry," Meilin said. "There's no excuse for disobeying and you can ground me later if you want, but that still doesn't answer my question. Why couldn't I see Connor—I mean, Hong Hai-Er, for who he really was?"

"Perhaps because, subconsciously, you saw who you wanted to see—someone who was interested in you."

Meilin exhaled heavily. "I'm such a doof!"

"Why? Because you let your feelings get in the way of rational thought? Zhu Bajie said. "That happens to everyone every second of the day. You're no different. If you were, you'd be..."

"Like me," Xiao-Hong cut it in. She gazed at both Meilin and Zhu Bajie. It was an awkward moment. "You don't have to respond to that," she said, forcing a smile and taking them off the hook.

"The other possible reason you couldn't detect him is because he blocked your ability to do so," Zhu Bajie resumed.

"With some kind of magical force field?" Meilin said.

"Force field?" Xiao-Hong interjected.

"Another future thing," Meilin replied.

"You *are* from a strange time, indeed," Xiao-Hong remarked.

"You got *that* right!" Meilin agreed.

"Hopefully, you've inherited your father's ability to see through any guise—but until that power manifests, you'll have to depend on your gut instincts." Zhu Bajie said. "Now, you better get going before your mother finds us missing!"

Zhu Bajie conjured a cloud under his feet and flew off on his own mission.

"Wait! You still haven't told me how to fight him!" Meilin called.

"You'll figure it out!" Zhu Bajie replied, his voice trailing away. "Just remember, *'Mercy brings victory in battle and strength in defense. When you let go of what you are, you become what you might be.'*"

"Dang it, Uncle Z!" Meilin cried with frustration. "I don't need another fortune cookie saying! I need to know what to do!"

But it was too late. Her uncle was already gone.

There was a sudden commotion inside Water Curtain Cave. "Where is she?" Meilin could hear her mother call. "Meilin! Meilin!"

"The Princess, Zhu Bajie and the Huli-jing left the cave ten minutes ago," she heard a sentry reply.

"Oh my God! Guards! Find them at once!"

"Well, that's our cue," Meilin said, conjuring a cloud large enough for two. Within seconds she and Xiao-Hong were airborne, speeding their way southeast toward the land of the Fiery Mountains.

Meilin looked back and saw the tiny semblance of her mother, accompanied by her guards, racing across the monkey bridge that led from the cave.

"Sorry, Mom," Meilin muttered. "But I gotta do this."

Chapter 18

M eilin and Xiao-Hong flew on their cloud for several hours. Eventually the lush terrain below gave way to grasslands and then desert. After another hour of flight, the Fiery Mountains finally came into view. They were entering the kingdom of the Demon Bull King.

"We'll have to be careful," Xiao-Hong cautioned. "Even though Bull King is hiding in exile, his subjects aren't. They won't be too pleased if we cross their path!"

"I know," Meilin said, remembering her last encounter with the cow-faced demons that served Bull King. They were a despicable lot and quite crude. They were also capable warriors who could overwhelm their opponents with their sheer size and muscle. Still, they were no match for her father—or her on that day. But that was then, and this was now.

The Fiery Mountains spanned hundreds of miles and it would have taken Meilin weeks of searching to locate Hong Hai-Er's lair. But Hong Hai-Er anticipated that and left no question as to where he was. A single shaft of pure Samadhi fire shot up into the sky from the top of one of the many mountainous plateaus—a beacon, lighting the way.

It was late in the day when Meilin and Xiao-Hong touched down near the edge of the plateau. Even at such a high elevation, the Fiery Mountains lived up to their name. The heat from the fires that issued from the fissures in the rocks was unbearable. It was hard to believe that any form of life could reside in this abominable place—but it did.

Almost immediately, Meilin and Xiao-Hong were set upon by a score of snarling lizard warriors that crawled out from under rocks and crevices. They were vicious-looking demons, armed with razor-sharp swords and clubs.

"Looks like Hong Hai-Er isn't going to make it easy!" Meilin said as she drew her longest jade hair stick from her ponytail knot. The hair stick instantly morphed to bo staff size.

"His aim is to wear you down," Xiao-Hong replied, drawing her own weapons—two deadly short swords, from the sleeves of her robe.

"It's gonna take a lot more than these guys to do that," Meilin said, ready to meet their attackers head on.

As soon as she spoke, another score of demon lizards appeared from behind.

"Me and my big mouth," Meilin grunted.

Rather than let the demon lizards surround them, Meilin and Xiao-Hong split up, each taking one of the two groups individually.

Meilin's jade bo whirled with amazing accuracy as she pressed her attack forward. The lizard warriors came at her in two's and three's, but she easily parried their blades with her staff and disabled them with lightning-fast blows, first to their legs, then up to their heads, back down to their forearms or elbows with numbing blows to dislodge their swords or clubs, then back up to their heads to finish them off. But swords and clubs were not the only weapons in these demons' arsenals.

Several tried to sweep Meilin off her feet with their tails while others came at her spitting venom from their mouths. She easily evaded their tail sweeps with her demon monkey agility, vaulting over the lizards and then cracking them on the back of their heads with her staff before she touched down.

The fact that the demons could spit venom was a surprise to Meilin and she barely managed to avoid the deadly, sticky spray that the lizards spewed from glands in their mouths. But Meilin quickly realized that the demons could only spit once and needed time for their poison glands to replenish.

Meilin avoided the spray by either leaping backward out of range or by sliding on the ground underneath the poison mist. She would then shoot up and clock the lizard warrior under the chin with the business end of her staff, sending him flying.

Xiao-Hong was equally skilled at fighting. The demon fox took out lizard after lizard as she moved through their ranks, wielding her dual short swords with the expertise of a master. She avoided the lizards' venom by shielding her face and eyes with the wide sleeves of her robe, a move she incorporated into her slicing sword attacks that dispatched the demon lizards in rapid succession.

Meilin marveled at the fluid way Xiao-Hong moved. She was glad that the Huli-jing was on her side. She would be a formidable opponent.

The foray only lasted a few minutes. Badly beaten, the demon lizards retreated back into the crevices that they came from.

"Is that the end of them?" Meilin asked as she and Xiao-Hong regrouped.

"End of them, perhaps," Xiao-Hong replied. "But not the end."

The two resumed their path toward the center of the plateau, each wary now of every crack and crevasse in the terrain that could hide a potential foe.

In the distance, the beacon of Samadhi fire still blazed. Meilin estimated that Hong Hai-Er's blue flame was about two miles from their current position.

They continued their pace for another hundred yards when Xiao-Hong suddenly stumbled.

"What's wrong?" Meilin said anxiously. She grabbed the Huli-jing's elbow to steady her.

"Poison," Xiao-Hong replied. "Some of it must have gotten on me through my robe."

The Huli-jing immediately tore at her robe, ripping the sleeves off and throwing them on the ground. She checked her white-furred forearms. Some of her fur was discolored where the lizards' poison had found its way onto her.

"What do we do?" Meilin cried.

"We press on," Xiao-Hong returned.

"But you can't fight!"

"It'll pass!" Xiao-Hong insisted. She was still unsteady on her feet and her vision was blurring.

Xiao-Hong motioned that they should continue.

Meilin exhaled heavily and against her better judgment, did as the Huli-jing requested.

The pair didn't travel more than a mile before they encountered their next adversaries.

Two huge demon cows barred their way. One wielded dual long swords that he flashed about his body with terrifying speed in an attempt to strike fear into Meilin and Xiao-Hong.

The other held a huge rock in his hands.

"Stay here," Meilin said to Xiao-Hong. The Huli-jing didn't contest Meilin's command.

Meilin stepped forward and directly confronted the demon cows.

The demon cow that carried the large rock in his hands snorted wildly at Meilin. He then lifted the rock and smashed it on top of his own head. It crumbled to pieces on impact!

"Ooo!" Meilin winced. "That's gonna leave a bump. Need an aspirin?"

The demon cow's nostrils flared and he snorted again loudly, lowered his head, pawed at the ground with his hoofed feet and charged. He came at Meilin like a runaway locomotive, intent on ramming her with his head and running her through with his sharp horns.

Meilin dug her feet into the ground and readied herself for impact. When the demon cow was within striking distance, Meilin quickly arched her jade bo staff straight up and brought it smashing down square on the center of the raging cow's head, stopping him in his tracks, sending him face first, unconscious, to the ground.

"Nighty-night!" Meilin quipped.

Meilin then twirled her bo around herself, imitating the flashy taunt her remaining opponent did with his swords just moments ago—signaling to the demon, *your turn!*

The remaining demon cow mooed and charged, his two blades whirling like a dervish.

Meilin immediately shrank her jade bo staff to a shorter jo staff size so she could wield it with one hand. She dodged to the right while slapping the first oncoming blade to the side. She then raised the jo to block the second descending blade that followed the first. She let her jo deflect the blade and then moved inside, parrying the first as it came at her again. She then rotated her jo with her wrist and sent it smashing down on the demon cow's head, stunning him.

The demon cow mooed with pain as he jumped backward. Rage filled his eyes and he immediately charged forward again, this time arcing both his swords down at Meilin with an overhead lunging attack.

Meilin parried both with an outside block, grabbed the demon cow's left wrist with her free hand and twisted it to the side, exposing the demon's ribs that she struck hard with her jo.

Meilin continued her strikes to the demon cow's ribcage as she stepped behind, pinning the sword-arm she still controlled against his back.

The demon tried to wrest himself free by rotating his body while swinging his free sword arm in an effort to stab Meilin. But she was ready for the move and using her jo like a baton, intercepted his arm, gave it a twist and locked both of the demon cow's arms together behind his back. She then secured his arms by using her powerful demon monkey strength to bend and wrap one of his swords around his wrists, binding them securely together.

The demon cow mooed with frustrated defeat. But there was nothing he could do to free himself.

"Go home. Kiss your wife, if you have one. Play with your kids," Meilin whispered into his ear. "Do anything—be anything, but this!"

The demon cow glared at Meilin with utter disbelief before turning and stumbling down the road.

Sweat dripped freely from Meilin's brow, not from the fight, but from the intense heat.

"I would have killed him," Xiao-Hong remarked casually as she joined Meilin.

"Luckily, I'm not you!" Meilin replied, turning her face toward the Huli-jing and studying her. She could see that Xiao-Hong would have indeed done just that.

But Meilin knew deep inside, she wasn't like Xiao-Hong. She would *never* be like her. Meilin's mother was correct when she said fighting was wrong—on every level. *"Mercy brings victory in battle and strength in defense. When you let go of what you are, you become what you might be."* Her Uncle Z's words were clear to her now. Violence was completely against her Tao. But if Meilin didn't stand up for the innocent—the children, her people—they would die. *Yin is Yang, Yang is Yin, one flows into the other.* Meilin was determined to use whatever Yang she could muster to dispel darkness and restore harmony wherever she could. As long as she breathed, *that* would be her Tao.

Chapter 19

There were three more attempts made by small contingents of demon cow warriors and demon lizards against Meilin and Xiao-Hong before they finally entered the clearing where the Samadhi fire beacon blazed. Each time, Meilin easily repelled their assailants with her demon monkey skills and sent them packing. Xiao-Hong offered some help, but her blurred vision hampered her ability to fight effectively.

"Took you long enough," Hong Hai-Er said smugly to Meilin as she approached.

"We stopped for pizza along the way," Meilin returned. She gazed harshly at Hong Hai-Er and the fifty demon cow warriors that flanked him on either side.

"I thought this was between you and me," Meilin said.

"These guys? Hong Hai-Er smiled, gesturing to his guards. "They're just here to watch." Hong Hai-Er took a step forward. "I told you I wanted my world to see."

"We don't have to do this," Meilin said.

"Yes, we do," Hong Hai-Er replied coldly. "You know we do!"

"If you surrender, I'm sure the Jade Emperor's punishment will be fair."

"The Jade Emperor?" Hong Hai-Er laughed. "What a joke!" Then he added, "His fat butt won't be warming my father's throne much longer. But we're not here to discuss politics, are we!"

Meilin exhaled and shook her head slightly. "No, we're not."

Hong Hai-Er momentarily turned his attention to Xiao-Hong. "I like the look," he said, referring to her white fur. "Very becoming. Though I am surprised you're still alive. Guess foxes *do* have nine lives after all—no wait, that's cats. Never could get that straight. Well, no matter."

Xiao-Hong didn't respond. She just stared at him with her cold black Huli-jing eyes.

Hong Hai-Er returned his attention to Meilin. "Anything else?"

"One thing," Meilin returned. "Why the children?"

Hong Hai-Er looked at Meilin and then smiled his perfect Connor smile. "Why not?" was all he said.

Hong Hai-Er's hands erupted into blue flame. His palms quickly moved in a tight circle as he formed and shaped a large ball of Samadhi fire. He took a half step forward and launched the fireball straight at Meilin.

The Samadhi fireball rocketed toward Meilin at lightning speed. Just before it hit, Xiao-Hong leapt directly into its path. The fireball exploded against her chest and enveloped her in wild blue Samadhi flame.

"No!" Meilin screamed. But there was nothing she could do. Xiao-Hong was gone—completely incinerated.

"Monster!" Meilin cried.

"Now you're catching on!" Hong Hai-Er laughed. He formed another fireball in his hands and thrust it again at Meilin.

Meilin pulled her longest jade hair stick from her ponytail knot and morphed it into her bo as she dodged the incoming fireball by doing a back flip to the side. The Samadhi fireball missed her by mere inches.

Meilin knew she had to be careful. She wasn't impervious to flame like her father. One hit, and it'd be over for her.

Hong Hai-Er shot a rapid series of smaller Samadhi fireballs. Meilin used her bo like a double-ended baseball bat, smacking the fireballs straight back at Hong Hai-Er as fast as he shot them at her.

The deadly fireballs exploded on the ground around Hong Hai-Er's feet, causing him to jump back with frustration.

Angry, Hong Hai-Er pulled his sword. Immediately it erupted into a blade of blue Samadhi flame.

Meilin quickly pulled her two smaller jade hair sticks from her ponytail knot. She shrunk her bo in half, morphed her other two hair sticks to the same size and attached them to each end, creating a Chinese Sam Dan Bong—a three-sectioned fighting staff.

With an angry cry, Hong Hai-Er rushed at Meilin. Meilin readied herself, grasping the inside ends of the outer sticks of her three-section staff just above the joints.

Hong Hai-Er sliced diagonally at Meilin's head. Meilin blocked the fiery blade, batting it away with the leading section of her jade Sam Dan Bong.

Hong Hai-Er took a half-step back, arched his blade high and then down for an overhead strike, hoping to cut Meilin in two. Meilin easily blocked his overhead strike with the center section of her staff.

Frustrated, Hong Hai-Er came at her again, this time swinging horizontally at her midsection. Meilin twisted her body to the side and flipped her staff vertically, letting the center section again block his fiery blade. He cut wildly at her four more times, hoping that the shear force and rapidity of his blows would slice through Meilin's defenses, but Meilin spun from side to side, using the center portion of her staff to block each attempt.

Meilin then jumped backwards and used her three-section staff like a whip and slammed it into Hong Hai-Er's ribs. He cried out with surprise and pain as Meilin drove him backward, hitting him hard in the ribs again, his knees, and then with an overhead strike to his head that sent him to the ground.

With an angry roar, Hong Hai-Er regained his feet and rushed Meilin again. Meilin spun the leading end of her staff like a propeller, parrying Hong Hai-Er's lunges and swipes. She then straightened her three-section staff like a long bo and spun it around her body, then arced it up high in the air. She brought the business end of her staff down, cracking Hong Hai-Er on the back of his head and down his spine, sending him down to the ground. His fiery sword skittered from his hands across the dirt.

"Kill her!" Hong Hai-Er cried with frustrated anger and embarrassment.

Instantly the demon cow warriors drew their own swords and rushed toward Meilin.

"Oh, snap!" Meilin cursed. She should have known that Hong Hai-Er wouldn't play it straight. Fifty against one were rotten odds, no matter how skilled Meilin was.

Meilin pulled some monkey fur from her forearm and blew on it. "Multiply!" she said, hoping that the same magic her father used in the stories Zhu Bajie often told her as a child would work for her. It did.

Meilin replicated herself into a small army, thirty strong, complete with a replicated version of her own jade bo staff. Immediately the Meilin clones engaged the demon cows and quickly began to knock them out.

There were so many *Meilins* on the battlefield that Hong Hai-Er couldn't determine which one was real. He fired hundreds of fireballs at them all, some of them hitting their marks—more often hitting his own demon warriors. The Meilin clones he hit burst into puffs of smoke. The demon cows he hit burst into flame.

a few moments, all of Hong Hai-Er's
s were vanquished.

over!" Meilin said, facing him.

g Hai-Er was beside himself with rage. "No!
No! No!" he wailed.

He clenched his hands into tight fists and
tensed every muscle in his body. *I will have you!*
he hissed.

Suddenly Hong Hai-Er's entire body erupted
into blue Samadhi fire. Meilin's eyes widened with
disbelief. Hong Hai-Er had become a blazing
torch!

With a terrifying war cry, Hong Hai-Er rushed
at Meilin, determined to envelop her in his
burning arms.

Meilin attempted to fly backward, but the
Samadhi inferno was so intense that it created a
massive vacuum, sucking the surrounding air
into Hong Hai-Er like a tornado—pulling Meilin
directly into him!

There was nothing Meilin could do. She was
sucked toward Hong Hai-Er with such force that
even if she could morph herself into a bird, she
could not pull away.

With wild glee, Hong Hai-Er reached out to
encircle Meilin with his fiery arms.

And then Meilin was gone. Just before he had
her in his deadly embrace, a pair of white-furred

arms appeared from nowhere, surrounded Meilin and yanked her back—into nothingness.

Hong Hai-Er screamed with rage. He spun around and around. He had her! He knew he had Meilin—but she was gone!

"Ahhh!" he wailed as he turned in place again, determined to find her. Suddenly, he felt the searing pain of two short swords plunging into his back. The shock of the blades entering his body extinguished his flames.

Xiao-Hong fully materialized from the Shadow Realm behind him.

"That's for what you did to me in the forest!" Xiao-Hong whispered coldly into his ear. She withdrew her blades as Hong Hai-Er staggered forward and fell to his knees.

The Huli-jing spun her short swords in her hands as she advanced on him, determined to end his life once and for all.

But as she brought down her blades to finish the job, Meilin reappeared from the Shadow Realm and stopped her.

"No!" Meilin commanded, intercepting Xiao-Hong's descending blades with her jade bo staff.

"It's over!" Meilin said. "We've won!"

"It's not over until he pays!" Xiao-Hong spat. The Huli-jing raised her short swords again.

"I said, no!" Meilin restated, grabbing the Huli-jing's nearest wrist and staying her arm with an iron grip.

"We're *not* like him," Meilin said.

"I'm exactly like him!" Xiao-Hong countered.

"No," Meilin insisted, relaxing her grip. "You're not! If you were, you wouldn't have pulled me into the Shadow Realm to save my life."

Meilin stared into Xiao-Hong's cold black eyes. "You told me yourself that Huli-jings have no soul—that your kind surrendered to darkness ages ago. Well, I don't believe that. To change into your spirit-fox form and move in and out of the Shadow Realm requires both Yin and Yang. Otherwise you'd be stuck there forever. There *is* Yang in you, Xiao-Hong. You just have to relearn to embrace it. The path to enlightenment isn't closed to you—or any of your kind."

Xiao-Hong studied Meilin for several moments. And though her cold expression did not change, she relaxed the tension in her arms and stood.

A sickening laughter emanated from Hong Hai-Er's throat. "You are such fools if you think this is over," he spat as he rolled on his back. He glared up at them. "Even though you've defeated my Samadhi fire, you neglected one thing. I still control this mountain—and you'll never make it off alive!"

The ground beneath Meilin's feet began to tremble and shake. Within seconds, the entire plateau they were standing on erupted. Explosive forces blasted huge chunks of rock and debris high into the air. Fires and bubbling lava shot up through the crumbling rocks. They weren't standing on a plateau at all. It was a volcano!

Hong Hai-Er laughed maniacally as the plateau began to buckle and sink into itself.

"We gotta get outta here!" Meilin cried as she tried to conjure a cloud large enough to lift all three of them to safety. But the ground shook so violently that she fell to her knees before completing the spell. A huge fissure opened up in the ground they were on, spewing an ocean of lava straight at them.

Meilin saw death rushing at her with all the force of a molten tidal wave.

"This is it!" she thought. Meilin closed her eyes, centered herself, and thought of her mother. She wanted that to be the last image in her mind...

Then, just before the three were swallowed up, the mountain went suddenly still. The fires disappeared, the molten lava solidified and the scorching heat vanished.

A strong ice-cold breeze blew across Meilin's face.

How could this be? How could the devastating force of an erupting volcano be so suddenly quelled?

"Yee-ha!" Meilin heard in the distance.

Meilin opened her eyes and turned her head in the direction of the sun and saw Zhu Bajie flying toward them with a host of Celestial warriors. In Zhu Bajie's hands was a large banana leaf fan, which he waved vigorously in every direction.

"Uncle Z!" Meilin cried as he landed. She ran to him and hugged him close, never wanting to let go. Zhu Bajie hugged her equally close in return.

While the Celestial soldiers took charge and secured Hong Hai-Er with the same magical bands Guanyin bound him with six hundred years ago, Meilin stepped back, looked at her uncle and shook her head.

"Nice of you to drop in," she said.

"Well, I had to get this fan from Red Boy's mother first. It's the only thing that can put out Samadhi fire or quell Fiery Mountain. Princess Iron Fan didn't want to give it up, but I reminded her how your father got it from her last time and, well—here we are."

Zhu Bajie's eyes then narrowed. "You two all right?"

Meilin nodded and smiled. "We're fine," she said, taking one of Xiao-Hong's hands in hers and squeezing it tight. "Just fine!"

Meilin then turned her attention to the imprisoned Hong Hai-Er. "What's gonna happen to him?"

"That's up to the Jade Emperor," Zhu Bajie replied. "But hey!" he said, changing the subject. "Didn't I tell you to wait for me before you started anything?"

Meilin looked at Xiao-Hong, then back at her uncle. "No," she said with a shrug. "You hear him say that?" she asked Xiao-Hong.

"No," Xiao-Hong echoed, also shaking her head.

"I know I said it," Zhu Bajie insisted.

"No, you didn't!"

"Yes, I did."

"No—you didn't..."

"We'll settle this back home."

"Fine," Meilin said. "Doesn't change the fact that you didn't say anything."

"Did!"

"Didn't!"

"You're so grounded..." Zhu Bajie said.

"Don't care."

"Did!"

"Didn't..."

Chapter 20

"**I**'ve half a mind to bar you from ever using the Gate to come here again! Do you know how worried I was! If something had happened..." Lijuan's voice broke as she struggled to hold back her tears. She sank down heavily on Sun Wukong's throne. "If I ever lost you..."

Meilin went to her mother and threw her arms around her. "I'm sorry, Mom," Meilin cried. "I know it was wrong," she said, looking into her mother's eyes, "but I also know it was right. I know who I am now..." she said.

"Meilin! Meilin!" several tiny voices interrupted. Meilin turned as a group of the recovering monkey-children appeared with a shaman. They ran to her with outstretched arms. Meilin turned from her mother, went to her knees and embraced them all. Their tiny faces beamed with pure joy, in spite of their serious injuries. Meilin hugged and kissed each of them with all the love her heart could give. Their touch, their fur—it didn't bother her any more. Meilin really *did* know who she was. She turned her face up to her mother and Uncle Zhu and said proudly, "I am monkey!"

- - - - -

"If it isn't *chopstick* and her pet dweeb," Tiffany remarked as she and her posse approached Meilin and Jessie in the Midland Hills high school hallway.

Three days had passed since Meilin left school. During her absence, all knowledge of Connor Hunt seemed to have disappeared. Once his magical presence was dispelled, it was as if he had never existed. No one, except Meilin and Jessie, had any memory of him at all.

"Was hoping you moved away," Tiffany laughed as she and her clones waltzed by and headed for their lockers.

"You wish!" Jessie shot back.

"Did you hear something?" the girl named Mackenzie wondered aloud.

"Sounded like some kind of dog yapping," another of the Tiffany-clones replied.

"Someone ought'a call the ASPCA," Tiffany sneered.

"That's it!" Jessie growled, clenching her fists. She started to go after Tiffany and her clique, but Meilin stayed her.

"C'mon! You're not gonna take that from them anymore, right?" Jessie complained.

"Just wait," Meilin replied.

"For what!" Jessie grunted.

"You'll see..." Meilin smiled.

They didn't have to wait long. As soon as Tiffany spun her padlock and opened her locker door, one hundred large black and brown rats poured out onto the hallway floor. The rats quickly leapt onto Tiffany and her posse. They climbed up their legs, tugged on their hair and sent them frantically screaming about the hallway.

Jessie's mouth dropped open with amazement.

Meilin then waved her hand slightly and the rats disappeared, leaving the girls completely confused, disheveled and their collective hair a total mess.

Jessie turned to Meilin and saw that her friend had a small tuft of monkey hair in her hand.

"Oh, *you're* bad!" Jessie grinned.

"Just balancing my Tao," Meilin said. She then chuckled, "Eh-heh-heh," in her own monkey way.

Glossary

Guanyin *(guan-yin)* The Taoist Goddess of Mercy.

Hong Hai-Er *(honh hi ar)* Red Boy. Son of Demon Bull King and Princess Iron Fan.

Huli-jing *(huli jing)* A Chinese fairy fox-spirit trickster, usually female, that can be good or bad.

Lijuan *(lee-jewan)* Beautiful and graceful.

Meilin *(may-lin)* Beautiful jade or plum jade.

Mount Huaguo *(hwa-gwo-ah)* The Mountain of Flowers and Fruit.

Princess Iron Fan The wife of Demon Bull King and Hong Hai-Er's mother. Whirlwinds created by her magical banana leaf fan have the ability to control the flames of Fiery Mountain.

Samadhi Fire *(sah-may-dee)* Holy or divine fire. Samahdi is the state of consciousness induced by complete meditation.

Shuilian-dong *(shway-lee-ann dohn)* The fabled Water Curtain Cave. Home of the monkey kingdom.

Sun Wukong *(swun wukong)* The Monkey King [*Sun* monkey + *Wu* awareness + *Kong* vacuity, *Wukong* awakened to emptiness.]

Tao *(dao)* (in Chinese philosophy) the absolute principle underlying the universe, combining within itself the principles of yin and yang and signifying the way, or code of behavior, that is in harmony with the natural order. The interpretation of Tao in the Tao-te-Ching developed into the philosophical religion of Taoism. [The Way or Path.] It stresses humility, compassion and moderation.

Xiao-Hong *(Shao-hong)* Morning Rainbow.

Yang (in Chinese philosophy) the active male principle of the universe, characterized as creative and associated with heaven, heat, and light.

Yin (in Chinese philosophy) the passive female principle of the universe, characterized as sustaining and associated with earth, dark, and cold.

Yin Yang yin and yang are complementary opposites within a greater whole. In Asian philosophy, *everything* has both yin and yang aspects, which constantly interact, change and are never static.

Zhu Bajie *(jou ba-jeh)* aka Pigsy the Pig. An immortal turned into a pig-demon for breaking the prohibitions of Buddhism. *[Zhu* pig + *Ba* eight + *Jie* prohibitions.]

悠悠扎
You-You Zha
满族民谣

1. 悠悠扎，悠悠扎，妈妈的宝宝睡觉吧
（重复四次）
2. 白桦树皮啊，做摇篮巴布扎
3. 狼来了虎来了，吗唬子来了都不怕
4. 白山上生啊--黑水里长--巴布扎
5. 长大了要学那，巴图鲁阿爸巴布扎
1. 悠悠扎，悠悠扎，妈妈的宝宝快睡吧
1. 悠悠扎，悠悠扎，妈妈的宝宝快睡吧

1. 悠悠扎，悠悠扎，妈妈的宝宝快睡吧
1. 悠悠扎，悠悠扎，妈妈的宝宝快睡吧
4. 白山上生啊--黑水里长--巴布扎
5. 长大了要学那，巴图鲁阿爸巴布扎
1. 悠悠扎，悠悠扎，妈妈的宝宝快睡吧

You-You Zha
(a Mandarin lullaby from Northeast China)
Pin Yin and literal English translation
by Gang Liu

1. Yōu yōu zhā, yōu yōu zhā, mā ma de bǎo bao shuì jiào ba.   *(repeat 4 times)*
Hush, mommy's precious baby, go to sleep. *(you you zha doesn't mean anything—a regional expression meant to lull a baby to sleep.)*

2. Bái huà shù pí a, zuò yáo lán bā bù zhā.
White birch's bark, (let's) make a crib (from it).

3. Láng lái le, hǔ lái le, mā hǔ zi lái le dōu bú pà.
Wolf coming, tiger coming, demon coming, be not afraid.

4. Bái shān shàng shēng a, hēi shuǐ lǐ zhǎng, bā bù zhā.
You were born on the white mountain, and grow in black water.

5. Zhǎng dà le yào xué nà, bā tú lǔ ā bà bā bù zhā.
When you grow up, learn from the hero hunter Ba Too Loo.

Within the spirit of the song and with some literary license, it is presented in this story as follows:

"Hush, little baby, go to sleep... In your cradle of bark from the white birch tree... Even if a wolf, tiger, or demon comes, have no fear... High in the white mountain, where the water runs deep, you are safe... When you grow up, you'll become a hero."

To read more books in the series and follow

THE MANY ADVENTURES OF MEILIN

THE MONKEY KING'S DAUGHTER

visit your favorite bookstore
or log on to:

themonkeykingsdaughter.com

5921843R0

Made in the USA
Lexington, KY
27 June 2010